Greetings From Charmaine Gordon

Welcome dear readers. Enter into my imagination. I'm here to invite you to visit River's Edge where Kindness to Strangers is the Motto.

Wouldn't you love to live where neighbors look out for each other, where children play outside without fear and no elaborate play dates have to be arranged. I sure would. Like the good old times where widows weren't widowed very long because friends were busy match making. And neighbors made soup for the ailing sick friends at home.

A place to call home reminding me days gone by brought River's Edge to this author's mind and creative juices flowed. Add pets to the mix and what do you have? A homey portion of Americana where anything is possible.

So put your feet up and enjoy the read. I wish all of you good health and love,

Charmaine Gordon

River's Edge Trio

Volume 1

by

Charmaine Gordon

Vanilla Heart Publishing

River's Edge Trio
Volume 1

by Charmaine Gordon

Copyright 2014 Charmaine Gordon

Published by: Vanilla Heart Publishing

www.VanillaHeartBookAndAuthors.com

10121 Evergreen Way, 25-156

Everett, WA 98204 USA

This book is a work of fiction. Names, characters, places, and incidents are either the product of the author's imagination or are used fictitiously, and any resemblance to places, events, or persons living or dead is purely coincidental.

ISBN-13: 978-0692331712 ISBN-10: 0692331719

10 9 8 7 6 5 4 3 2 1 First Edition

First Printing, November 2014

Printed in the United States of America

She Didn't Say No

by

Charmaine Gordon

Dedication

She Didn't Say No could not have been written without the help from my daughter, Amy Malone. With patience and care, she researched and answered my questions the way I've done for her in all our precious years together. This is not the first time Amy sorted out a story with me and it won't be the last. Thank you, my one and only daughter. This story is for you. Love, Mom

Acknowledgements

Thanks to Kimberlee Williams, the best publisher ever, for her encouragement to this less than computer savvy author.

If you listen to words of wisdom and follow the lead, you can't go wrong. Thanks for support and friendship to said Ms. Williams and to Chelle Cordero, always there with a helping hand. And to Angela Kay Austin who listened to me when we first met, I'm happy we've remained close friends.

Chapter One
1960. A year full of promise

I focused on studies; my goal to be a veterinarian required concentration and high grades. The library emptied most Saturday afternoons as the campus prepared for dates, parties and events that had nothing to do with me, a country girl from way upstate New York with ambition and parent's expectations of greatness from their only child. One student, I'd seen him before, a guy called a BMOC, Big Man On Campus, glanced over from another table and grinned.

"Hey, you. I've seen you a bunch of times before with your cute little nose in the books. Don't you ever come up for air?"

Me? He spoke to me? This handsome guy, captain of the swim team said my nose is cute.

Next thing I knew, he plunked books next to me and grinned again.

"Scott Dwyer." He extended his right hand, muscles rippling through his white tee shirt.

I tentatively reached over to shake it and he pulled me closer. "Don't be afraid. I don't bite."

Grasping his hand with a firm grip, I shook it. "I'm not afraid of anything. I'm Grace Meredith. Now I must finish this chapter before the library closes."

"What's your goal, Miss big brain. You're young to be graduating this year. How did that happen? Did Daddy pay off someone?"

I stiffened, wanting to smack his face. "Hey, not that it's any of your business but I've been an accelerated student all the way through school and I've earned my way to graduate by studying."

Hey, Grace, I'm sorry. I'm not stupid even if I am a jock. I heard you were nineteen and I had to meet you for a lot of reasons."

Curious, I wanted to hear the reasons why the BMOC even thought about me at all. "Reasons?"

He tilted his head, a blond curl fell across his forehead. Counting on his fingers, he held up a thumb. "Number one—you're different from the other girls, not flirty and teasing all the time. Number two—you have a style all your own and I admire that. Number three."

"Stop. You're embarrassing me." I wanted to hear more words pour from this handsome boy who made me mad and now I liked him.

He grinned. "So what's your goal with all this," he gestured to the heap of books on the table, "all this uh, studying?"

"I plan to be a veterinarian. How about you?"

"Law with a strong leaning toward criminal justice."

"Like FBI or Police Academy?"

He frowned. "Not sure. It's all so far away but maybe I'll specialize in the K-9 Corp. See, we both care about animals. We have something in common."

He sat back and appeared to be very pleased with himself. I liked his self confidence, something I lacked even though I'd boasted about not being afraid of anything. Right. My parents frightened me with their expectations and pressure. A buzzer sounded signaling time's up at the library.

I slammed the book shut and jumped to my feet. "Scott, how about playing hooky from studying and let's go to the beach."

Did I catch a surprised look on his handsome face? "I'm with you, Grace. Just so happens I have a car."

"Oh." I blushed. I hadn't thought about getting there. Today I'd walked from my small apartment close to campus. "Cool." And we were off on a late spring afternoon in 1960 driving in a shiny yellow Volkswagen Bug.

He zoomed down the road laughing when the scarf I'd tied over my hair blew off and landed in the back. "Your hair is pretty blowing around in the wind."

So this is what it's like being with a guy, I thought. Having fun and a little flirting. He sure had experience talking. He's the pretty one, not me.

We went to Nyack about a half hour north of school and parked at the hiking section. "There's a small beach a little way up over some boulders. The Hudson River is darn cold right now but beautiful." He gave me another half grin, grabbed a blanket from the trunk and we climbed a short way.

Goose bumps rose on my arms from the breeze blowing across the water. No jacket and I'm shaking. What an impression to make on this guy. And suddenly Scott wrapped his arms and the blanket around us and we were all alone. Body heat warmed and overwhelmed me with a yearning I'd never experienced before.

"Better?" His voice had deepened. He rubbed my arms.

"Yes. Much better. I should've worn a jacket."

The kiss, tentative at first, made me tingle all over. I'd never had a boyfriend before. This feeling was new to me. Too busy being the obedient daughter appeasing my parents demands on time to experiment at being a kid, a teenager. So here I am at nineteen not knowing what to do with a first kiss, for God sake.

"Well, uh hi Scott. You're a um, good kisser."

Laughing, he hugged me tight. "Only good? I can do better than that." This time the kiss curled my socks and knocked me for a loop.

Gasping for breath, I yelled, "Bingo." The wind carried my word across the river and boomeranged back for an echo. "Bingo, bing, bin."

Sitting at the edge where sand meets water, sheltered by some boulders Scott asked me about my background. I said, "You first," certain he'd grown up in a house with a picket fence, smiling parents, siblings and lots of relatives. All true as his fairy tale life of twenty one years unfolded.

"I hope I didn't bore you, Grace." He planted a kiss on top of my straight brown hair. "Do you realize how pretty you are and the way your eyes match your hair? They're so dark and mysterious. Are secrets hiding behind there?"

Giggling, I nodded. "I'm nineteen. Never been kissed 'til you."

Frowning, he looked across the river and seemed to think about what I'd said.

"That's a big responsibility but I can handle it. Now tell me about your life."

Without meeting his eyes, I told him everything, how my parents ruled my life up in Buffalo, NY and allowed me to attend this school far southeast from them for the first time with high expectancy for success. So far so good since my grades were outstanding. Best of all I had money my sweet grandfather left in an account no one else could touch but me."

"Oh." Scott held me close and I pictured other girls cuddling up in his arms. "Tell me about your grandfather. I have both sets of grandparents still living. Lucky for me."

I had to smile at Scott's interest and told him of my stern grandfather who melted whenever he saw me. "Scott, we

14

didn't have a big family like you do so the fact that my grandfather cared for me and showed he loved me and I could fly into his arms and he'd whirl me around and laugh was one of the few real joys growing up. Mother would try to stop him. He never listened."

"What did he do? I mean his work?"

"He was a banker who worked himself up to CEO and president and without telling my parents, made out his will leaving everything to me. His top financial advisor contacted me privately after the funeral and set up a plan where the money would grow and I'd be independently comfortable for the rest of my life."

"Wow. That's quite a story. Thanks for telling me." His arms went around me and I felt safe. "Let's have dinner somewhere close and head back to the campus. Okay?"

"Sure." I prayed he'd want to see me again, to hold and kiss me some more but first dinner. One step at a time, I cautioned. I had a few more years of school to get a veterinarian degree, probably at Purdue and he had major plans for his future. Right now, with his warm hand high on my thigh, I couldn't think clearly.

After burgers, fries, and milkshakes he followed my directions to my apartment. Looking up at the nice building, he smiled. "So you live here. I've passed this place like a zillion times never thinking the girl of my dreams might be right upstairs."

"Girl of your dreams?" I smacked his shoulder. "You probably say that to all the girls."

"No, Grace. I mean it. I've admired you for months at the library and here we are."

Is this where I say come up or what? And then I heard myself asking if he'd like to come up and we were inside and kissing in my quiet apartment where no one ever came. Ever until now. I always wondered what happens when two young people are alone, hormones raging. Hearing about it and reading books is not the same. I wore a spring sweater set, pleated skirt, underwear, socks and sneakers. Nothing sexy except my feelings and wanting him. Scott had experience on his side. Was I expected to be a casual lay? I didn't know and didn't care.

First we sat on the couch and necked. That led to touching and stroking each other and then , oh so politely, he asked if I minded if he did this and that and soon we were naked on my maiden double bed with pink flowered sheets and a matching spread.

"Grace, you're so beautiful." He fondled my breasts as if they were treasures and tasted one nipple and then the other. And sucked like a baby searching for milk. My hands grabbed his head, ran my fingers through his thick curly hair and held him close never wanting him to leave me. My first lover. My only love. "Do you have protection?" Protection? Um, oh birth control.

"I have a diaphragm and cream but I never used it." It occurred to me this was a funny conversation in the heat of nakedness.

"Oh. Well, this time leave it up to me. Next time practice until you get it right because I have a feeling we're gonna need a lot of protection." He groaned and I heard a rip of a packet and fumbling and soon he played with the dark moist space between my thighs until I lifted my hips to heaven. Slowly, he entered the virgin territory where only a tampon had been. No comparison here as he continued to move in a little deeper each time to break the barrier and we were one reaching for the stars.

So this is what all the fuss is all about, I thought. And I wanted more and right away. Like a demon possessed, I coaxed his wilted member into an upright position after about half an hour and we lost count by night's end collapsing in each other's arms.

Vowing to love each other forever, finish school in a few years and begin a life together, we became the hottest unlikely new couple on campus. The studious girl and the BMOC. School first the priority. We made a promise not to interfere with our different plans. I'd be off to Purdue and he hadn't solidified his plans yet. Law schools offered scholarships for the brightest students; pick one. He'd almost made up his mind since graduation was in June, a couple of months away.

A month later I missed my period. Always on time, first I worried and kept it to myself and then frantic, I told him a big fat lie. Crossing my fingers and hoping to die for what I was about to say, I called my dearest love. "I'm sick with the flu and don't want you to catch it." Busy with finals, Scott said okay and he missed me and hoped I felt better soon and we'd be together again. I sniffled and said yes to my first and only love.

By the second late period, I was sure. Skipping classes and having someone bring assignments to my apartment, I completed my work. Making a list of pros and cons, I faced the facts. By now, I'd cried too much pacing the floor alone with no one to talk to and afraid I might hurt the baby with all my grief, I reached for an inner strength to move on. Heartbroken, the practical side of me decided Scott must never know. I couldn't burden his life, ruin his career with a baby. As for me, I'd go to Buffalo, tell my parents and they'd help me solve the problem.

My dearest Scott. Tears fell. Ink ran. I started over many times until the well ran dry, crumpled paper littered the floor and I wrote:

My Dearest Scott,

I'm saying goodbye. Not because I want to but because I have to. Our paths are too divergent to survive the long wait until we can be together. You must go your way and I have to go mine. Please know you are my one and only love. I wish you well. Have a good life. And, and I don't know what else to say except goodbye.

Grace.

The letter made no sense. Choices made with no guidance. Choices that changed our lives forever.

Packing all my belongings including books, I gazed around the only place I'd found love and happiness for a short time. I made the long drive from St. Thomas Aquinas University up to Buffalo in a new two door Pontiac I'd bought a few days ago, my first car thanks to my generous grandfather. All the way northwest I thought about the baby. Above all I want her or him to feel peaceful and calm. I won't let anyone stand in the way of my baby's happiness. Naïve when I think back.

Gutsy and determined I parked in the driveway of the home I'd grown up in. No joy here, I thought, but surely my parents would help sort this serious situation out for me, their only daughter. I opened the door with my own key and called, "Mother, are you home?"

"Grace, what are you doing here?" She took one look at my loose jeans and tee shirt and stepped back.

I could tell. She knew. Her lips tightened in a thin line. It was a 'wait until your father hears about this' moment. How dumb to come home. They wouldn't open their closed hearts. I'd disappointed them. About to shame them to their friends and now they would hate me. I heard the silent accusatory words in my mind. "We'll never be able to hold up our heads in the community or in church if word gets out you're pregnant. Abortion or go away and give the baby up for adoption." Parents are supposed to guide their kids and I need help right now.

Without a word, I left. I wiped sweaty hands dry on a loose tee shirt and drove, and finally stopped at what appeared to be a well kept small town. A wide street with no debris blowing around and aromas coming from Betty's Home Cookin' Diner. The diner smelled of home cooked food as advertised. Hungry, I ordered vegetable soup and toast, nibbling on crackers until a steaming bowl arrived. Plans. I had to make plans for our future. Listening in on conversations around me, I hear two girls talking about a Dr. Feldman who delivered so and so's baby and what a great guy blah, blah, blah. My ears perked up and I scribbled his name on a paper napkin. Using the phone booth outside, I called his number to speak with the secretary. A kind deep voice answered.

"Hi. I just came to town and need to see Dr. Feldman right away. Is he in like now?"

"I'm Dr. Feldman and yes I'm here. What seems to be the problem? Can you wait until office hours tomorrow?"

"Oh." I wanted to cry. He sounded so nice and , and uh, patient. "Sir, it can't wait. I can't wait. Please."

He gave me directions and I drove to his office at the back of a house with a white picket fence, purple hydrangeas in bloom and a bed of all colors of tulips just like the ones Scott had described about the house he's grown up in. So warm and homey. I rang the bell and heard the bark of a large dog respond.

"Now Maggie, we have a young lady visitor. Be a good girl." Dr Feldman greeted me with a warm smile, a white female sheep dog with short clipped hair stood at his side. "Are you afraid of dogs?"

"Oh no. I wanted to be a veterinarian and now I think my plans will have to change." I held out my hand and Maggie sniffed. I pointed down. She hunkered down. I signaled stay. She stayed.

"Impressive. Obviously you've had a lot of training or you've studied hard." I nodded. "The reason for your call is not about dogs, I assume."

"Yes sir. I think, I know I'm pregnant and I hope you'll confirm it."

"Why me?"

I searched for an answer by checking out his diplomas and pictures. Finally I spilled the beans. "No one knows. My boyfriend loves me but we, well he has a few years of law school ahead and I can't burden him with a baby so I didn't tell him. Maybe it's wrong of me to decide for him but he's a good guy. He'd say yes and throw away his future. My parents turned their backs on me so I'm going to have my baby and raise her or him by myself. And that's what my plan is."

We looked at each other for a long time. "If you don't want to help me, I'll drive 'til I find another doctor." Standing, I picked up my bag. Maggie stood too and got in my way.

"She's herding you. That's what she does. Do you mind telling me your name?"

Should I lie? What if there was an APB out for me? "Grace."

"Grace, if you were my daughter, I'd give you different advice but since your mind is made up, for now, let's have a look to make sure. It's the very least I can do.

After the examination, I dressed and met Dr. Feldman in his office. His smile seemed sad. "Yes, you're about eleven weeks pregnant. I have a bottle of pre natal vitamins here for you. Take one a day and when you get settled, find an obstetrician. Meanwhile," he handed a paper to me, "here's a good diet to follow. Eat healthy, low fat foods, low calorie, veggies, fruits, juice. In other words, follow this diet. You won't regret it." He walked me to the door. "Take this card and don't lose it. If you need advice, change your mind, or just want to say Happy New Year, please do."

I knew we'd never meet again.

"I know you're not coming back, young lady" He patted my hand. "Whatever it is you're running from, find roots in a thriving town and start fresh. I have a good feeling about you. I'd truly like to see a Christmas card from you every year. Drop a line to say you're feeling fine."

I left not wanting to shed a tear and hit the road after swallowing a vitamin with water from a fountain in the park across the street. While having the tank filled before I left the town, I asked for a map of New York State. The filling station wasn't busy and the owner came out to chat.

"What're you looking for?"

He had the feel of a man who'd been there forever but it turned out he'd come up northwest from Brooklyn to find peace in the country.

"I want a nice town to start a pet grooming business." Where did that come from? I wondered. Veterinarian dreams already faded to a simpler more manageable kind of business yet I'd still be with dogs and cats. Yes I'd have a lot to learn but I recalled you could learn the how-to as an apprentice or take classes for certification. My mind worked faster than my mouth just then. "In your travels, did you ever come across towns you thought might be appropriate for a person starting out on her own?"

He stuck out a hand for me to shake. "Jack Connor, here. All alone, huh?"

I shook his hand and shrugged. "Tired of college and being bossed around by the folks back home. Callie Feld." The name popped out so I went with it.

"Well Callie, there's a nice area of towns where there's waterfalls 'n creeks not far from Rockland County. Just far enough to be real pretty and small townish, if ya know what I mean. One I always liked is River's Edge. You might check that out. See if they have pet groomers there. I settled here 'cause my wife wanted to be near her people. It's been good for us and the kids."

SHE DIDN'T SAY NO

He made some marks on the map circling the area. I thanked my helpful new friend, Jack, paid the bill and drove on. Breathing deeply, thankful for kind people, I let go of anger toward parents who had no time to care for or understand me.

Chapter Two
Moving on

The kindness of strangers along the way. That's what helped me on the path to my new home. Nineteen and pregnant but I had money enough to make a good start for us. I found the town and there were no pet grooming businesses nearby. Without much trouble, I smiled my way into a realtor's office and told the receptionist what I needed. With a skeptical look, she buzzed someone and after a few minutes, a gray haired tall man came out.

"I'm Jim Trumbull. Please come in."

Uh oh. He's the boss. The company's name was Trumbull Realty. I needed to rev up my confidence factor and appear to be sure of myself. Well, I am confident, damn it.

I smiled bright and sweet. "I'm new in town and I want to buy a place big enough to establish a pet grooming emporium with an apartment for me above or maybe behind the property."

He blinked a few times and polished his glasses. "Your name is?"

"Sorry." I grinned. "Grace Meredith."

"Miss Meredith, the property you request may be very costly. Do you have the means?"

"Do you have such a property, Mr. Trumbull? If so, I'd like to see it right away or you may have a few suitable for my specifications. Then we can discuss my means, as you call it."

He leaned back in his chair and laughed so hard his glasses fell off and clattered to the floor. Picking them up, he mopped his eyes dry with a handkerchief. "Let's go, young lady. I do believe I have the perfect place for you and your pet emporium.

Coincidence, karma, fate or all of the above brought me to River's Edge that day. I'd had enough bad luck in my life and now a new beginning. Mr. Trumbull drove me a few blocks from his office. We could have walked but I guessed this was the way he treated clients. A corner lot with a building loomed ahead. He parked. We got out. My heart beat faster as I surveyed what to my inexperienced eyes, appeared to be two lots with one cozy looking building constructed of natural wood not exactly a cabin; more like a big cottage.

Don't appear to be too excited, I thought. I wanted to twirl around and dance. I couldn't negotiate a price if I showed eagerness so be cool, Grace. Let's see what's inside.

"The owner, Doctor Daly, had a good veterinarian practice here for years. He retired a few months ago and moved to Florida. We all miss him. Let's go inside."

It was a sign. Pets had been here. A veterinarian. I felt it in my bones and heart. Oh baby, this is the place.

Doctor Daly left the place clean inside. I wandered around touching everything to picture what I'd need for my purpose. I climbed the stairs to follow Mr. Trumbull's lead. The apartment up there was plain, not meant to be a real living space but okay for now. Bathroom, small kitchen, again all clean. I'd need a good carpenter.

"Seen enough, Miss Meredith?"

"I'd like to check out the yard."

"Follow me and be careful."

A high pioneer fence guarded the yard with a dog run on one side and flower beds in bloom everywhere. An old majestic oak tree grew in one section.

24

"How much?" I couldn't help myself from asking.

Again he laughed hard enough to set birds flying. "You're supposed to play hard to get, Miss Meredith."

Oh, Mr. Trumbull, that's how I got in trouble. I didn't say no soon enough.

Grinning, I said, "It's perfect for me and my uh, business. Now we negotiate, right?"

Ever the gentleman, he took my arm to guide me through the yard, cottage and the front path back to his car. Instead of the office, he drove to a restaurant just outside of the town's limits. River's Edge Fine Dining. "This is the best restaurant for miles around. People come up from New York City to dine here."

A good looking man greeted Mr. Trumbull. A black Labrador Retriever stayed at his side secured by a lead. I offered my palm to the dog. He sniffed then licked with obvious enthusiasm.

"This is Grace Meredith, Larry. She's a dog person who intends to open a pet grooming emporium right here on Main Street." Mr. Trumbull introduced me to my first client before I had a shop or anything.

"Jim, you've brought Grace to the right restaurant. Dinner's on the house to welcome a soon to be member of the Chamber of Commerce. I'm Larry Owens, Grace. And this is my hunting dog and best pal, Spike."

"May I pet him?"

"You seem to know what you're doing. Go ahead."

"Come, Spike." I opened my hand. He took his time and approached.

"Good boy." I used the squeaky voice dogs love. Kneeling, I pointed to the ground. He sat and again lavished kisses enough to warm my heart. "Spike, you're the best." Long strokes from head to tail sealed the deal. Spike and I bonded.

"Good show, Grace. Spike doesn't respond to strangers. There's a nice table outside in back so you can get your first look at the waterfalls we're known for."

Overcome by kindness and hospitality, I first went to the ladies room and washed up, added lip gloss to an otherwise pale face. Hungry and tired after the long journey from Buffalo and back I wondered what came next. Pinch me if it all went well, I thought and went outside.

Mr. Trumbull sat, a folder opened next to menus. Water cascaded to the rocks below creating an echo to bounce off the sides of huge boulders along the banks of a stream.

All of a sudden I felt small and too young and inexperienced to be a mother, a business person, a mother, a, well anyone except a student taking tests alone in a small apartment on a campus. I could end this charade, this pretense by throwing myself over the balcony onto the rocks. How foolish to run away and think I could raise a baby, start a business all by myself.

Mr. Trumbull's hand warmed mine. "Grace, speak to me. I'm a good listener."

The kindness of strangers. I told him my whole story. More than he needed to know. We had soup between little segments and by the time we had the main course of broiled salmon, so delicious with steamed spinach just like on Dr. Feldman's diet, I'd finished.

Patting his lips, he set the napkin aside. "We have a three-fold problem to solve. You need a good obstetrician and I know just the doctor right here in town and after the baby's born, you'll need. . ."

I gasped. My hands flew to my belly. "How did you know?"

He moved his chair closer. I hoped he didn't want our conversation to be overheard. "In order to be successful in my business, I learned long ago to study people. Every so often you stroke your tummy in a protective or soothing motion. I've seen this before and knew." He touched my hand. "You have nothing to fear from me, Grace. Try to keep calm and listen. Deal?"

"Okay. I'll try and it's a deal." I breathed in through my nose for an eight count, held for eight and exhaled through my mouth the way the best phys ed teacher ever taught my first year at college. After a few times, I calmed and listened as agreed. As he spoke, I recognized experience and authority in his voice.

"The Emporium must be fitted for your purpose and you'll need hired help. At least two capable experienced dog and cat lovers. You might want to begin with just dogs to keep it simple while the baby is young. And you will want to be a certified groomer to enhance your respectability. I'll help you check into that. And a number one priority is a proper apartment upstairs for you and yours." He rubbed his hands together, a smile tugging at the corners of his mouth.

"Sounds overwhelming. It is overwhelming. I must be nuts to think I'm capable of doing all this alone." Again I watched the waterfall pound away at the rocks wishing I could escape. How did a simple life get so complicated? Choices, Grace. You made choices.

"You don't have to, Grace. The past few years have proved to be shocking and ultimately left me bored. My son Ryan flew the coop and moved out west. My wife decided she didn't want to be married to boring James Trumbull, Realtor anymore and divorced me. And suddenly you marched into my life like a ray of sunshine with determination and guts to take on an impossible job. I'd like to be your partner in business, Grace Meredith. What do you think about them apples?"

ChapterThree
The Partnership

Wonder of wonder, miracle of miracles, Jim and I drew up an uncomplicated plan, easy for me to understand, boundaries clearly defined. Insisting I needed a lawyer, he gave me a list of several in town. Closing my eyes, I picked one. He chuckled, said what a great choice and made the call. Perry Crain arrived within an hour. Meanwhile Jim called a bed and breakfast up the road and booked a room for me. He also called a Doctor Bergen and after a friendly hi and how are you, made an appointment for me to see her tomorrow.

I curled up on a leather couch and watched years drop away from the man I'd met a few hours before. His brown eyes twinkled with energy; every movement he made was like a more youthful man about to begin a journey. Closing my eyes, I dozed to wake when my lawyer, soon to be friend, arrived.

"Sorry to disturb you, Miss Meredith. Jim called and said you needed council. I've been known to lull courtrooms to sleep but not before we've been introduced."

How adorable, I thought. Balding with a white fringe, crinkles around his eyes and mouth from laughter not frowns as far as I could tell through sleepy eyes. I liked Perry Crain at first glance.

We had the privacy of Jim's office to us while Perry read the agreement and explained it to me before I signed. "This is a fine partnership you've gotten into. Jim doesn't usually trust many people to get close so I'm surprised. You two have been friends along time, I assume."

I smiled thinking if a few hours is a long time, the answer is yes. It's magic. Serendipity. Luck.

"Your fee, Mr. Crain?"

"Jim holds a marker with my name on it. This settles the score. If there's anything I can help you with in the near future, please call. Best wishes in River's Edge, Grace." He handed me a card. "I do have dogs. Two of them. Labradoodles in need of grooming and training. They're young. I realize you won't be set up for business for a while but are you willing to make a house call?"

Is water wet? Does a bear poop in the woods? "Since I just got here, my appointment book is almost clear. How about after breakfast tomorrow? I'm staying at the Bed and Breakfast nearby. If someone is home, I can come over and check out your dogs. I love Labradoodles. They're smart."

"Does ten a.m. work for you? My office is at home so I'll be there. Call if there's a problem." We shook hands. Perry Crain left and I twirled around. My first house call! I'll look up the chapter on those curly haired wonder dogs and be ready for them.

"Jim, are you here?"

"Of course. Where else would your new partner be? How did you like my old pal Perry Crain?"

"He's great. You're great." I began to cry. "It's like a dream. Tell me it's really true, Jim."

"Oh, Grace. It's true. I don't know how come you and I met; what set of circumstances set you on this collision course with me but it's real and all good. I'm so grateful. We have an opportunity to bring new life to this beautiful town."

"In more ways than one." I laughed and patted my belly. "Hey, I'm making a house call to Perry Crain's pooches tomorrow. Seems they're out of control and need a bit of Grace training."

He grinned. "By the book?"

"By the biscuit."

Chapter Four

Waking with a tear soaked pillow case in my new home at Miss Mollie's Bed and Breakfast for the next short time, I sat up disoriented recalling the endless yesterday and all the events that led me to River's Edge. Running away from college and Scott leaving him an incoherent dishonest note. Since when did I lie? Now I'd add that to my sins. No wonder Mother threw me out. And then my luck changed and person by another kind person led me here. I washed the pillow case and myself from top to bottom making a fresh start on this early summer morning. Today I had my first client. Lawyer Perry Crain's puppies and I would get acquainted but first I had to read about the breed and know what to expect.

After breakfast, I thumbed through several of my dog books and found the information needed. Read and reread, make notes was the only way for me to remember so that's what I did.

At ten, heart hammering just like facing a test, I walked down the path to the Crain's door and knocked. A tearful woman opened the door attempting to restrain the puppies.

"Hi, I'm Grace Meredith. I spoke to Mr. Crain last night and he's asked me to see about training your Labradoodles."

She clutched her heart. "Oh thank heavens. They're adorable but out of control. We have no experience with pets and they were supposed to be trained." She gestured to them running around and barking. "I guess the breeder lied."

"Their names?"

"We call them Schnaps and Shtrudle."

"Ah. Do they know their names?"

"Hmm. Come to think of it, no. They just run around and only come to us when food is placed in their bowls."

"Might you and your husband consider giving them simple names? Easy to understand."

"Oh definitely. Anything to make life pleasant. We looked forward to these cuties for a long time and now." She raised her hands palms up as if in frustration.

"Okay. Say the first dog name to come to mind."

She looked at the ceiling, gazed around the room and settled on a card table. "Ace."

"Oh. I like it. And another."

"Deuce."

"You like to play cards." She nodded. "Leave us alone for a while and we'll get to work." An hour later, Mrs. Crain peeked in the room where I literally had Ace and Deuce eating out of my hand. Doodles are an intelligent breed and it didn't take much to train them. They responded well to hand signals and verbal commands rewarded with small biscuits I'd bought at a pet supply shop on Main Street. Not sure as to what I'd charge, I first took the dogs through their paces and had Mrs. Crain follow me a few times. The puppies fell asleep after the workout and many wet smooches. Definitely another shower was needed before the appointment with the obstetrician this afternoon. I loved working with them and when the lady of the house got all weepy and asked me to return for another session to reinforce today's lesson, I agreed. She peeled off fifty dollars and handed it to me. Not knowing what the going rate for a house call was, I thanked her and made a date for the following day.

Wait 'til Jim hears about this, I thought. I bought a ledger at the stationery store to keep expenditures and gains for tax purposes. Grace, you are a woman with a business head. Who'd a thunk it? as they said up in Buffalo.

With my head held high on a June afternoon when I should have been marching with classmates to graduate from St. Thomas Aquinas University, I began a new life leaving the past   behind.

32

Chapter Five

Doctor Lorraine Bergen greeted me when I entered a comfortable waiting room for my first appointment. "So you're the young woman Jim called about. He's very impressed with you and warned me to take excellent care or else." Her smile lit up the room filled with wooden toys in one corner, magazines in another, and an array of tea, soda, and a water cooler stand with cups and saucers. Everything one needed to feel at home while waiting. Cozier than home ever felt to me, I thought. "Follow me, my dear. Samantha, my nurse called in sick so it's just us chickens today. We'll manage." She flashed another smile. I walked behind her and checked out the graceful way she moved, like a former athlete, posture perfect, and a long gray pony tail bobbed along to her arms swinging back and forth. I felt like a little blob in the wake of a speedboat.

She handed me a gown. "Please remove everything and I can give you a thorough examination."

Left alone, panic set in. So far I hadn't said a word, no papers to fill out, insurance stuff. Jim promised he'd keep my secrets and I believed him.

"Ready or not, here I come."

Still fully dressed, I burst into tears.

"Grace, I'm here to take care of you, be not only your doctor but your friend. Please trust me to do my job. I'm very good. That's why your pal Jim called me. Blink your eyes once for yes if you understand."

I blinked once and giggled and giggled some more.

"That's better. Now let's start fresh. Clothes off." She checked her watch. "I have one hour to be with you. Let's make it a productive one. We'll take care of paper work next visit.

Fast, gentle, efficient. A good description of my new doctor.

"It's no surprise to both of us that you're about three months pregnant. Any nausea, morning sickness?"

"No. Um, Doctor, I ran away from my boyfriend so he doesn't know. We were about to graduate college and we'd known each for a few months so I didn't want to ruin his long term plans and I just left. Without giving him a choice." Afraid to look in her eyes, I chewed on the knuckle of my right thumb.

"Look at me, Grace. Do you really think you're the only girl in the world who faced this decision?" She leaned across the desk saving my thumb. "I did the same thing."

"You did?" Incredulous to learn this educated strong woman was once a kid like me, I almost felt relieved.

"I'm not going into details but I look at you and see me at nineteen and I'm amazed at the similarity between us. So stop biting your thumb. You'll need it for work." She rattled a bunch of notes and shoved them aside. "Ms. Grace Meredith, without checking blood work since Samantha isn't here, I find that you are in spectacular good health. Next visit, in three weeks, we'll continue to monitor you and the baby's progress. Here's a bottle of pre natal vitamins. Take one a day."

"Dr. Feldman gave me a bottle two days ago. He's from a town northwest of here. We met when I was searching for a good safe place to settle."

She jumped out of her chair, ran around the desk and hugged me. "He's a wonderful man. I learned a lot working with him years ago. You keep the vitamins; there's more where that came from, Grace. Now get out and take care." She stopped me with words of caution. "River's Edge is a marvelous place to live in. Beware of gossip and don't take it seriously. Remember we're living in a relatively small town."

"Thanks for everything. I'll call tomorrow for an appointment. See you in three weeks." Gossip, huh. What did that have to do with me?

Chapter Six

Jim and I worked together for part of every day after that first incredible afternoon. The good doctor's words came back to haunt me when I realized the whole town gossiped about the once staid realtor they knew who seemed to be to carrying on with the chick from nowhere.

At the diner one morning, Mimi the owner, walked over to a booth where two women were pointing at me and shaking their heads. In a strong voice, she said, "You don't like our coffee today, ladies?" I didn't know who they were but I knew they had it in for me. The words 'morality' and 'good example' came across loud and clear. Mimi said, "Grace and Jim Trumbull are partners in business at the new Pet Emporium to open real soon" The women snickered. I finished a late breakfast, paid the bill, touched Mimi's shoulder and left. Small towns and gossip. I wasn't prepared for this. As my pregnancy developed, tongues would surely wag at the coffee shop, the bars and every other hang-out for miles around.

Over breakfast at the diner one morning, I saw the same nasty women. Jim greeted them and introduced me. "This is Grace Meredith, my new partner. We're in the midst of rebuilding Dr. Daly's old building into a Dog Grooming business. Grace, this is Dorothy Warren and her sister Laura Warren, President of the Chamber of Commerce." The sisters nodded and murmured hello in unison. A formidable twosome. No kindness of strangers here. They stared at my blossoming middle. We walked to our booth dodging bullets or slings and arrows.

"Don't worry about them. They never married and seem to be content with their positions as town gossips. To know you, Grace, is to love you."

Love me? I wondered and dropped the thought like a hot potato. Jim is twenty years older than me. We're just friends or is something more going on? "Has our partnership hurt your real estate business?"

"If anything, business has improved. My educated guess is folks want to check out the old guy who has a young pregnant girl on the side. They want to be near all the power and hope it rubs off."

We had a good laugh over the image of Super Jim the realtor. I intended to buy him a tee shirt with a big S on the front but somehow the days and nights flew by.

Hungry as always, I hurried to Mimi's Diner for a supplemental breakfast only to regret my decision as soon as the door closed behind me. Loud words spoken by Dorothy Warren carried across for all to hear and aimed at me. "What qualifies you to groom our dogs?"

Thank God for Jim's advice about me getting certified as a Groomer. I enrolled in a certification course by mail the day after I came to town and old study habits kicked in. And I thought college kept me busy. Real life doubled the effort without grades and tests. And now the finished, approved papers were in my backpack and the certificate was at the framers ready to be picked up and hung as soon as the shop, our shop opened.

I kept my cool and smiled to one and all. "I'm a certified Groomer with papers to prove it. If you have pets, know they'll be safe at the Pet Emporium."

Mimi's voice boomed out kitchen doors swinging behind her. "Hey Grace, my bulldog, Roscoe needs an overhaul. Soon as you open, I'll bring him in."

Support from Mimi meant a lot in town. "I make house calls, Mimi. Ask Perry Crain." Waving thanks. I slid into a back booth and ordered chocolate milk and a slice of apple pie. Not quite the diet Dr. Feldman had recommended but sometimes a woman just needed somethin' sweet. A lotta sweet to cover the sour taste left of non-stop gossip. I feared those sisters weren't finished with me and would continue to dig and poke. Be on your guard, kid, my inner voice warned. Be ready to counter-attack at all times. In life there's always the good with the bad.

I felt a stand-off coming soon at Mimi's Diner. Every time I walked over there, the Warren's came in right after me or were already seated in a booth ready for another confrontation. I didn't intend to cross paths with the likes of them. Conflict. How I disliked it after cowering before my parents all my young life. No more, I thought. Too many people thrived on it. This situation required a discussion with my best pal and partner.

On site while carpenters did their thing with our venture into business, Jim and I found boxes to sit on.

"What's up, Grace?"

I sighed. "Gossip is up. The Warren women are using Mimi's Diner to cause trouble and I can't seem to avoid them. So I appeal to you, my friend." Did I catch a gleam in Jim's eyes when I said those words? Hmm. Be careful of personal involvement. Keep it strictly business.

He cleared his throat. "They are wicked, those two. Laura Warren won't be able to block your nomination to the Chamber of Commerce. You already have several creditable members who sent letters in recommending you and all you need is two. I counted four and more are forthcoming. But, and here's the big BUTT!"

The last word started laughter as hard as waterfall hitting boulders on the stream. We couldn't stop. The carpenters joined in. They never missed a word despite the hammers and saws making a racket. I wiped tears from my eyes and sipped water to get control.

Jim caught his breath and continued. "They must have a spy."

"A spy?"

"Oh, yes. Someone at the diner is sending a Grace alert when you leave here to walk over there."

"Hmm. It figures. It must be the cashier. She has the best view of the street."

"Right. And I've heard she needs extra cash since her husband is out of work so whatever they're paying her is important."

"How sad, Jim. What can we do? This is real life, not a novel for fun about two spiteful women. Maybe he could work here as a handyman to take up the slack and, and oh, we could ask Mimi to dark curtain one side of the street view so the cashier can't see me until it's too late. Oh, blinds. Wood blinds might work." I thought for another minute or two. "Jim, I need a script, like words to say if I'm confronted again otherwise I'm going to say, "Shut up you nosy bitches and leave me alone."

He appeared to agree and then burst into laughter joined by the workmen. "Way to go, Grace. I'll work on it."

Opening day at the Emporium: Special opening day free box of dog biscuits announced in an ad in neighboring newspapers had the phones ringing. I pictured future customers clipping coupons for biscuits if they came in. My assistants and I wore red and blue dog paw print designed smocks. Both Petra and Mike had years of experience, way more than me. I learned from them and I was the boss!

Jim stayed in the background to take notes and say hello if anyone noticed him. "I don't want to steal your thunder, partner. Not on your big day."

Hugging him tight as I could get with my rounder than ever belly in the way, I almost cried. "We've accomplished all this in such a short time, Jim. And you've made me a part of your community. Thank you like, uh forever."

"Forever is good, Grace. My plan is to live a very long life and to be here for your baby to teach her what I know, see her graduate, get married." He smiled. "All the good stuff. Now greet your first customer with a dazzling smile and talk to the dogs in the high pitched voice I've heard you use." It was then I realized our friendship had grown into a love affair without the sexual undertones. As yet.

"Hi, I'm Grace and these are my trained assistants, Petra and Mike. Welcome to the Pet Emporium." Mike kept the records on the first day; each pet's name, breed and age, owner address, and more while Petra led the dog to a grooming table, talking to the pet in the high voice I'd practiced with my capable assistants. Fur flew, scissors snipped, brushes of different sizes were replaced and cleaned after each pet. Grooming included a wash, ears cleaned and nails clipped. Some customers wanted nail polish on their poodles. Yikes! The day ended with the last bark of approval as I leaned down to whisper in a sad Saluki's ear. She licked my face after a minute or two and perked up when I used long soothing strokes from her sweet head all the way down her back over and over again.

"You whispered to her! Wait until I tell my husband. He wanted to send her back because she just sat around so quiet." Tears filled the woman's eyes." What can I do to help her?"

"Remember she's part of your family. When you take her for a walk, don't talk on the cell phone. Talk to her. Use a higher pitched voice as if she's a baby. Tell her you're proud of her and love her. We're about to close for the night, Mrs." I signaled Mike for a name, "Mrs. Brewster. Bring this precious pooch back to us again and here's a box of nutritious biscuits for a treat."

"Oh I will. Betsy needs obedience training. Do you do that?"

"Yes. We've had great success with some frisky puppies." The doodles came to mind; my first clients.

Doors closed and locked, Mike crunched the numbers and we all did a happy little dance including Jim who turned out to be the best dancer of all. My man of many talents. After splurging on pizza, everyone went home and I had quiet time to go upstairs to my cozy apartment almost finished except for baby furniture. Five months went by and the Pet Emporium business boomed. I didn't fit in our designated smocks anymore and waddled around in a long tee shirt covered by an apron. Some disguise. Everyone knew I was pregnant. Even the dogs. Some serious sniffing went on and they had to be coaxed into the tubs where before most of them couldn't wait to be washed. When Jim didn't have a showing, he spent time at our shop taking over when necessary. While resting my feet up on a chair one afternoon during lunch break, I saw Jim stride in with a Labrador Retriever on a lead.

He bent down and kissed my cheek. "This is Butch. He's a former K-9 dog injured and healed, now retired at way too young so I figured he'd make a good companion for you and the baby. He's just three and needs a good home, Grace." This time he kissed my lips. "We all need a good home."

"Jim, are you proposing something here?"

"I am. I have a large empty home and it needs to be filled with love by you, the baby, Butch, and me. Marry me."

Petra and Mike returned to find us deep in conversation. I told them to take over while Jim and I went for a walk with Butch who limped a tiny bit but seemed strong and obeyed on command. The day had turned cold as winter approached with leaves blowing all over to land in heaps against shop windows. My hood flew back and Jim tied it under my chin. I shivered at his touch. I did love him for many reasons but marriage? Lose my independence? Maybe a compromise where we might live together in harmony in his comfortable home without vows? Scandalous thought but why not?

"Let's go to your home and discuss the situation."

Without another word, Jim guided me toward the big Lincoln he drove. In the back I spied a dog bed, kibbles, and a blanket for Butch. The Golden dog hopped right in as if he'd done this for years. "You planned this, you big wonderful man." I kissed him and slid carefully in the passenger seat, mixed thoughts racing around in my muddled mind.

Driving to the residential part of River's Edge, we were quiet, an unusual state for both of us to be in. He pulled into a long driveway, opened a two car garage door, and drove in. We walked around to the front. "First I'll take Butch for a quick walk," and they disappeared toward a stand of leaf-less trees. I stamped my feet to keep them warm and soon they appeared both looking pleased. Then with a flourish, Jim opened the front door.

"Oh." I gasped at the beauty of the well kept old house, scented with lemon polish, gleaming cherry wood furniture, logs ready to be lit in the huge fireplace. Comfort and beauty combined made my small apartment above the shop seem insignificant by comparison. I pictured the baby growing up here, legitimate with a father who loved her and I almost ran from room to room like a kid touching, embracing everything and finally turned to the one most important person who followed me so patient and quiet.

"Jim. I do care for you and love you and I will marry you right away. And we will raise our little girl in this house as best we can with Butch as her protector and companion. Now show me to the bedroom right now."

Chapter Seven

A romance to remember

"It's been a long time for me, Grace. I uh, don't know if I remember how to. . ."

"Oh, hush. You're forty. That's a young man, not even middle age." I helped him undo the buttons of his shirt and didn't care if his muscles didn't ripple like an athlete. Knowing his feelings for me, how he'd taken me under his capable arms and made me his partner the first time we met; that's what counted. We were a perfect fit despite a twenty years difference. I'd been old since growing up in my parent's stultified atmosphere where childhood meant nothing.

"Honey, I don't have much experience either so let's wing it and do what comes naturally."

After a tentative beginning, Jim and I found each other and did the dance of love, careful not to disturb the baby inside. The sweetness of it all being wrapped in the arms of my lover and soon-to-be husband. Fragrant wisteria scented lotion, my favorite, poured first to warm in his big hands and gently Jim spread it over my body beginning with my shoulders and moving down. Between my fingers and over the swelling where he smiled as the baby gave a kick and roll. My breasts were more than a handful now and he paused to admire them rubbing a bit of lotion then tasting everywhere. Pausing lower, I urged him to go on lifting my hips feeling heat inside and when his erection pressed against my thigh, reached for it marveling at the size.

"Oh, Jim. You are one hunk of a man. My man." Almost incoherent with desire, I moved him in place and felt skin against skin for the first time without the barrier of protection. "Deeper, deeper, sweetheart." He filled me completely and made me want to sing at the top of my voice but I knew the spell might break so I gasped and loved every moment. When release came and it did for both of us, we curled up in a comfy spoon position and napped to wake later with a bark from the latest member of the family. Butch needed attention.

Jim grabbed his robe, a big blue terry cloth one in need of repair or the Goodwill basket, and stumbled downstairs after our dog. Our dog, I thought. Our home, our baby, our new life. All good. A fleeting thought of Scott Dwyer passed through my mind. He must be in school somewhere, arms around some campus cutie. My one and only love no more, replaced by a fine man. I prayed Jim and I had many good healthy years ahead of us to raise precious Cindy and give her the love I never had except for once in a while from my dear grandfather.

After the necessary documents were filled out, Jim and I were married at the Justice of the Peace in town witnessed by our lawyer Perry Crain and his wife Crystal. We celebrated at River's Edge Finest, inside this time. The bride, that's me, wore a white lace tent and white new sneakers. Laughter as we toasted. They drank champagne. I had white grape juice. Larry Owens stopped by to join us and picked up the tab. "I would have been flower girl or ring bearer if you'd called. Oh well. The christening is on you." More laughter. A few kicks and rolls from inside and I settled down to eat slowly and enjoy our wedding dinner.

After closing one evening, I climbed up on a ladder to straighten the star at the top of the Christmas tree. I remember watching snow fall thick and heavy enough to cover bushes on the walkway just before water flowed between my legs. Jim had warned me not to climb or do anything strenuous. Stubborn as always, I chose to do it my way.

"Help. My water broke. Someone call Jim. Call Dr. Bergen." No one answered. I forgot the staff had gone home. Alone I hung on tight to the ladder careful not to fall and reached the floor to walk through the puddle and call Jim.

"Help. It's time, Jim. Should I call the police?"

"I'll take care of you, dear Grace. Hang on and breathe just as we practiced."

My good doctor and friend after what seemed like endless months of pregnancy, Lorraine Bergen, stayed at my side through ten hours of labor and delivered our red faced beautiful baby.

Cindy Scooter Trumbull gave a war cry as she entered this world and hasn't stopped since that epic moment. James Trumbull became daddy to his sweet girl and taught her with wisdom and kindness all the days of his life.

I remembered kind Dr. Feldman and located the business card he'd given me on that fateful day. All he asked for in return was a holiday hello every year.. I scribbled a note about the good luck I'd found in River's Edge and my new partner in business and marriage and our baby girl. This became a tradition for a long time until one year my Christmas greeting was returned. Sadness filled my heart. A connection broken.

Chapter Eight
One day at a time

"Once upon a time," Jim rocked our three month old baby as he read a bed time story. Every night we hoped for a peaceful night's sleep. Her blue eyes closed and he kept rocking for a while longer. His eyes closed too and his head slumped forward. I lifted pink bundled Cindy from him and propped her on her side in the nursery next door to our room. Butch padded in after me, circled three times in his dog bed and settled down to guard his small charge. Now to rouse Jim and put him to bed; a mother's work is never done.

"Honey, time to go to sleep. Quick before she wakes up. Again. Maybe this night she'll sleep right through."

"Right through 'til two in the morning. My time to feed her then or yours. I forgot."

"Mine." I dived under the covers and passed out. No time for romance or a kiss goodnight.

We marked the calendar the next morning, astonished after a double take at the clock. Our precious girl had slept from ten at night 'til six in the morning. A milestone. She sapped all our energy for the time being and now, as the saying goes, we could see a glimmer at the end of the tunnel.

I didn't trust anyone yet to care for her so off we went each morning, baby needs packed in a carrier, and I worked.

Petra and Mike always helped out but the Pet Emporium had grown in six months and the possibilities seemed endless.

Mimi from the diner hurried over one morning, a woman in tow behind her. "Grace, this is Rachel Brown. She's a baby nurse, just retired from St. Paul's Hospital three towns south of here and she wants to continue working."

After thanking Mimi and promising her a zillion free sessions with Roscoe, her bulldog, my attention turned to Mrs. Brown.

Love at first sight. One look at the white haired woman with the kind pale blue eyes and I felt a kinship. Somewhere in my woe be gone background, Mother must have hired a pleasant woman to take care of me for a while and here she was, reincarnated to help raise Cindy. I showed her around the shop and the apartment upstairs, introduced her to Butch and finally he allowed her near the baby.

"I want Jim, my husband, to meet you, Mrs. Brown."

"Call me Rachel and you are?"

"Oh, uh, I'm so excited. I'm Grace. Grace Trumbull. Do you have a place to live? We have a large house. Comfortable, lots of room and well, you'll see that is if you'll take the job and live with us like forever."

Rachel laughed. "You'll want to check my credentials and give me a trial run."

"I will? Oh yes, of course, I will. Get Jim on the phone someone, please."

And after Jim walked over to see what the fuss was all about, we sat down like grown-ups and struck a deal. Life settled down after dear funny Rachel joined the family. She became like a wondrous character in one of my favorite stories from childhood; the story of Mary Poppins, a British series about a special kind of nanny.

Chapter Nine
Cindy's questions

Content to play with toys and all of us at home, once Cindy started pre-school at three she returned asking questions. "How come I don't have cousins like Susie?" Or "How come I don't have a baby brother, sister, auntie, uncle, grandma's and grandpa's?" She missed relatives no matter that she had a loving daddy, mommy, Rachel, and Butch. She wanted more. I knew the feeling to some degree. Jim and I discussed it with me pacing the floor wringing my hands feeling inadequate again.

The voice of reason prevailed when he said, "She's acting out. In truth, Cindy has more than enough so don't worry. We're not going to adopt a child and we agreed one is enough with both of us in business."

One day when she was four, she came home with the last straw that literally cracked my sense of sanity.

"Mommy, what's illa, um, I can't remember the bad word Lena called me."

Tears rolled down her smooth rosy cheeks and broke my heart. My past had caught up with me. Someone at pre-school said she was illegitimate. Gossip begun when I moved to River's Edge rose up to hurt my child. My hope that by marrying Jim before she was born, Jim legally became her father and Cindy would be protected from stigma. But no. Small town gossip never died. It smoldered for a while and erupted years later. My inner lioness roared and reawakened to protect my cub.

Drying her tears, I offered a chocolate chip cookie. Lower lip trembling she turned it down and climbed on my lap, her legs dangled, baby fat long gone. She looked just like Scott, I thought, with his blue eyes, curly blond hair and athlete's build. "Do you know Lena's last name?"

"Lena Warren. Dummy, stupid Lena, Meana. Call her mommy and tell her not to say that word or I'll." She made two small fists and punched the air.

"Rachel needs you to help walk Butch now, honey. I'll call the school and get Lena's phone number." She grabbed the cookie and ran through the house, Butch at her heels calling for her pal, the baby nurse who came and stayed to join our little family. Of course I called Jim. I felt his outrage at the insult to our child through the phone.

"Lena Warren is the kid's name. She must be related in some way to those sisters who tried to make life miserable for me five years ago. A cousin's child or distant relative since they were spinsters, old maids, bitches."

"Damn those women. I'll do an immediate check on who the relative is and get a number. This must be stopped before it goes any further. Grace, don't jump the gun. Let me get the information and we'll write a script just as we've done before. Many times. We want this to be a bloodless coup."

I laughed. Better than crying. Ever since he figured out those women paid someone to spy on me about five years ago, Jim loved to play detective.

With nothing to do for a few minutes, I paced the kitchen, opened and closed a lot of cabinets and found a box of Mac and Cheese. Water boiled just like the blood boiling inside me. No simmering for me when I thought way back to the short time when I never said no to Scott Dwyer. On the other hand, I wouldn't have this beautiful daughter and my darling Jim and my whole life changed all because I never said no.

I stirred and waited for noodles to cook and the phone to ring. I read the box as if it were news to me. At least four times a week the preferred meal for my kid. Cut the packet and pour in the cheese. What a cook. The phone rang. A quick cover jammed on the pot and I picked up on the second ring.

"Okay, Grace. Sit down but first turn off the burner."

"How did you know? Am I so predictable?"

"Not you. Our daughter is. Mac and Cheese, right?"

We shared a laugh and his tone grew serious. "It seems long ago Dorothy Warren married for a short time and her husband, an unsavory guy with jail time needed to escape from her so they divorced while she was pregnant."

"Hmm. Secrets unveiled."

"More. Much more. She gave the baby up for adoption but when a distant relative, you were so right, heard about said baby, he and his wife adopted the child, a boy. There's the connection. Now Mark Warren, adopted child all grown-up has a little girl named Lena."

"Who goes to pre-school with Cindy. Jim, how do we nip this before it spreads? My impulse is to go to the source, Dorothy, and tell her we know about her baby, gossip etc and."

"Or go to Mark Warner, tell him we know about his past and we insist he stop his kid from maligning our child. Hmm. He may not know he's adopted. Let's do it your way. I'll get the less than Honorable Miss Warren to come to my office for a little chat. Join us at," she heard him sifting through papers, "four today."

"How do you know she'll be available, Jim?"

"The Shadow Do." And he did an impersonation of a spooky laugh from a long ago radio program he'd told her about.

She hung up laughing. Cindy, Rachel and Butch transformed the house when they stomped in, cheeks rosy from an outside romp and tail wagging, the Golden Labrador Retriever had a goofy smile on his long doggy face.

They washed their hands and sat for a sumptuous feast, their faithful companion's background chomp and slurp to accompany the meal.

I hurried up to check on a decent wardrobe for the occasion. No more the pregnant kid from nowhere, Grace Trumbull was the impressive owner of the Pet Emporium and wife of the prominent realtor in River's Edge, James Trumbull. The soft grey wool suit would do. Short jacket with a little flare below the waist and a skirt that hung in a few unpressed pleats. Just right for me said the New York City saleswoman at Bergdorf Goodman Jim insisted we go to. Forehead bangs changed my straight brown hair to a new look. Silver hoop earrings gave the finishing touch and by four I sat in Jim's inner office, legs crossed, waiting for Dorothy Warren.

The voice pierced the air before she barreled in. My insides quivered. "What's this all about, Jim? What could be so important you had to drag me away from my knitting circle this afternoon."

"Calm down, Dorothy. We have a major problem to discuss with you."

"We? Who's we?" And then she saw me at the conference table, sipping hot tea in an attempt to appear in charge.

"You know my wife, Grace."

"Yes." She spun around. "I need coffee, lots of sugar."

Jim poured a fresh mug full of what she requested. A plate of cookies were on the table. Like a greedy child, she grabbed two.

We sat in silence while Dorothy settled in. Then Jim began. He started with the name calling at pre-school and the offender's name, Lena Warren caused her eyes to widen. "The name Warren reminded me of you so I did a bit of back-tracking and found that you're related to this child. Our daughter is not illegitimate. I am Cindy's father." I.Do.Not.Want.Our.Child.To.Suffer.From.Gossip." He gave her a wicked smile. "Do you understand, Dorothy?"

"No. What the hell are you talking about?" She stood so quickly, coffee spilled all over the front of her skirt. Jim slid napkins across the table and gestured for her to sit. She did.

"We know about your marriage to a man with a jail record and then your subsequent divorce, giving your baby away for adoption to a relative." Her face turned pale. "There are no secrets, Dorothy and gossip is mean. We can spread this news, true news not made up the way you smeared Grace when she first moved here. We can and will if you don't go to Mark Warren and his wife to tell them their little four year old daughter Lena has started to slander our Cindy. She heard the word illegitimate somewhere and my educated guess is it came from you."

She cried. "I want my sister and I want her now."

Jim and I exchanged glances and shrugged. "Call her if you must. It won't change any thing. This is up to you, Dorothy so fix it. That's your specialty. Grace and I will keep your secrets. But I warn you," Jim stood and towered over the woman who had caused me so much grief. "if we ever hear one mean word about our child's heritage, we'll go after you."

Still sobbing, Dorothy Warren grabbed a few more cookies and her handbag and slammed the door.

We sat silent for a while. "You're scary when someone crosses you, Jim."

"That's how I sell more real estate than anyone for miles around. Now get over here and sit on my lap."

Chapter Ten

The first stroke happened when Jim and I were walking with Butch through the snow one night. My husband stumbled. The cold wind blew snow around and I reached up to make sure Jim's scarf still covered his neck when I found him staring at nothing, one side of his mouth sagging. Oh God, please no. "Jimmy, talk to me, sweetheart." He turned his head and mumbled incoherently. Slowly I guided him back to the house and called for Rachel who came running down the stairs. "Help me. Help us."

"What's going on, Grace?" One look at my husband and she said, "I think he's had a TIA. I've seen this before."

Removing Jim's outerwear, Rachel led him to the living room to lie down. Unsteadily using Rachel's support, he somehow got to the couch and collapsed. With her expertise, she arranged him in a more comfortable position and turned to me after I called Andrew Blake, our family doctor and good friend.

"What's a TIA?"

"Transient Ischemic Attack. Minor stroke. Is Doctor Blake coming right away? Otherwise we'll call 911."

The doorbell rang. Andrew Blake must have used his son's cop car with flashing lights. "Andy, Jim's in here."

Wrapped in a warm blanket on the couch lay my bewildered husband lost in a fog we couldn't penetrate. I hovered nearby while Andy performed his magic and finally nodded saying the same words Rachel said a short while before. "Jim's had a TIA. There must be a blood clot that broke loose slowing the blood flow to his brain temporarily. It's essential for him to be seen by a top neurologist right away. I'll make a call and get someone to examine him tonight. The best and closest care right now is nearby St. Paul's in Lincolnshire about twenty miles south. An ambulance is on the way. This is a crucial time after TIA's to hopefully prevent further strokes."

He paused, exchanging a worried glance with me. My darling in danger. Out of nowhere, walking in the snow on a winter night, life reminds you how fragile you are. A grain of sand on the beach of life.

"Yes, I'll pack a" The siren of an ambulance split the air.

"No need to pack now. The hospital has everything Jim needs for tonight. Follow us there."

"I'm going with Jim."

"You'll be in the way, Grace. Get in your car and drive carefully. Rachel, you'll keep the home fires burning and don't worry Cindy. Jim's going to be all right."

After kissing Jim and assuring him I'd be at his side soon, I watched my precious husband being lifted onto a stretcher and out the door in falling snow. Always on top of everything, Rachel handed me a bag she'd packed with amenities if I stayed overnight. "I'll call when I know something more. When Cindy comes home tell her. . ."

"I'll figure out something close to the truth, Grace. Tell the good folks at St. Paul's I'm a member of your family. They'll take extra good care of our Jim."

The words further strokes repeated in the whirl of my mind spinning round and round all the way to the hospital.

An MRI showed a clot in the carotid artery dangerous enough to cause a more serious stroke. Dr. Bernstein, a well known neurosurgeon, friend of Andy Blake spoke freely to

Jim and me after another of a series of examinations. "Your brain has to cool for thirty days before I can operate."

I winced hearing about Jim's brain having to cool.. It sounded so science fiction. "Meanwhile don't do anything strenuous like shoveling the driveway. Gentle sex is all right." Jim flushed red in the cheeks and I thought, Yay! Better than nothing. "You're a young man." He looked at his chart. "Forty nine. I predict a long life ahead for you after this problem is resolved."

We made an appointment for the surgery in spring and pale faced I drove home, Jim beside me, thoughtful his mind clear.

"This is a big deal operation, Grace. I'll have a dueling scar down the side of my neck."

"Dueling? You don't know how to fence, silly."

"I mean it. Will you still love me with a scarred neck? Tell me the truth."

I pulled over into a small deserted park and showed him how much I loved him. When I finished and said, "There's more of that after the surgery, big boy," we continued traveling the familiar two lane road and reached our home. Cindy and Rachel had hung a long banner of Welcome Home, Daddy from all of us with hearts and flowers decorations. Somehow time had passed since the wintery night of the TIA and Valentine's Day approached. I shook my head in disbelief. Petra and Mike held down the fort at our Pet Emporium and Trumbull Realtor still rated number 1 in sales thanks to the faithful staff and good will of customers.

Jim, a grateful smile on his face, hugged Cindy. "How's school, my girl? Tell me all about your friends, teachers, homework and just plain stuff."

"Dad, you're so much better. I can tell. First, I have a boyfriend. I didn't tell you when you were sick but now I can, right?"

I waved to Jim over Cindy's head and mouthed okay with a thumbs up.

"Well sure. What's his name and does he like sports?"

Cindy's words spilled over to an interested father and I left the two of them to see what smelled so good in the kitchen. From now on we'd be on low fat or no-fat, fruit and vegetable, chicken and fish diet. Hmm. Sounded like my pregnancy routine. And no chocolate for nine months. What a pain!

Rachel pulled out the broiler tray with seasoned golden chicken filets and little red potatoes ready to eat. Steamed broccoli with a pat of better than butter, oh really? melting on top heaped high in a white tray. She rang the dinner bell.

"What's the good word, Grace?"

"Carotid artery surgery in a month."

"Well, we'll deal with that one day at a time."

And for the first time since that dreadful scary night, we all sat down for dinner together.

Chapter Eleven

"The surgery went well." the nurse said. "I'll bring you in soon to see your husband."

I paced the floor, waited and paced some more. Alone by choice, I had a book to read and never read. Two hours went by. Soon, she said. Two hours is way longer than soon. I cursed under my breath as relatives came and went everyone happy except for me. I called for a nurse, a someone in charge demanding to know what was going on.

"Mrs. Trumbull." I jumped up to face a starched older nurse. "There's been a complication with your husband."

"Complication?"

The operation went well but in the recovery room his blood pressure went high and then plummeted very low. Doctor Bernstein put in an emergency pacemaker to regulate his heart beat and now it's stable." She caught me as I slipped to the floor. Too much tension. She called for a glass of water. I sipped and recovered.

"He's all right? He's not going to die?"

"He's all right. You can see him right now. Please don't alarm him. You've both had enough trauma for one day."

She took my wrist and checked my pulse. My heart pounded. Slow down. Be strong. I can't. Yes, I can. "He's my rock."

Her kind eyes gazed into mine as if she saw the life I'd lived before I met Jim. "Now you be his."

Operations can change a person, especially anything to do with the heart and brain. Jim just had both and now he worried and waited for the other shoe to drop. I noticed his confidence wane as he spoke slower, softer, afraid of the effort to strain himself. Cindy was the only one he felt comfortable enough to be the old before-he-got-sick Daddy Jim. I became the cheerleader in the house, bouncing around like everything was cool. Finally I ran out of steam and brought a puppy home. Just what we needed to boost spirits, this three month old white with brown whiskers Wirehaired Pointer worked his way into our hearts the first day. Jim came out of his shell to begin life with a fresh attitude.

Butch tolerated the pup we named Boomer because he launched himself from one place to another and wore himself out to snuggle beside our old dog. No need to buy another bed for Boomer. He slept curled next to his furry master until sadly Butch departed a few years later.

Every month Jim had a date by phone with someone who called to check his pacemaker and make sure it still worked well. The phone rang right on time. He'd pick it up to verify his name and number and place the phone against the place on his chest where the pacemaker was implanted. He'd hang up, grin with a thumbs up and we'd breathe sighs of relief. Except for my husband's regimen of pills three times a day, mild exercise and a healthy diet, our little family adjusted well.

Until hippies came to town. On the outskirts of town, a group of young men and women formed some kind of commune. They dressed in torn jeans and loose gauze shirts made in India, I thought, after seeing one close up. The women were bra-less, said oh wow a lot, wore flowers in their hair and the guys wore head bands and earrings with feather or gold studs. They opened a run-down shop at the end of Main Street and sold their wares.

Parents were called to the high school for counseling about drugs. Drugs? In River's Edge? Watch out for strangers hanging around the school peddling marijuana, we were warned. JUST SAY NO posters hung from every lamppost. I read a book written by Peter Benchley titled Jaws and all I could think of is "just when you thought it was safe to go into the water." Kids wanted to try something new, something parents objected to. Our Cindy, busy with gymnastics and piano lessons, never mentioned drugs. I wondered if I should bring it up or wait and see. And then the worst happened. Cindy's close friend, Amanda Cummings who suffered from asthma tried marijuana, choked and died before help came.

Sadness enveloped our town. Hippies disappeared in a cloud of smoke never to be seen again. We were scarred from the loss of one of our own. Both kids and parents grieved and eventually flowers bloomed, snow fell, seasons changed and we survived. I never had the talk about drugs with my daughter. Never had to. When graduation came, a space was left to honor the memory of Amanda Cummings.

Our daughter went on to graduate college and Law School.

Jim reached out and touched my hip one night. A tentative loving flow of heat went from his hand to my body. In the quiet of our home, we could carry on like wild lovers but that time had passed with his illness taking a toll. Heart medications changed a person. Our romantic love slowed to a crawl. I longed for more and settled for less because we cared for each other.

"Grace?"

"I'm here."

"I love you."

"Prove it, big boy." Soon we were a tangle of bed clothes and sheets like in the old days. I kissed his mouth, cheeks, neck, to work my way down to the pacemaker where I planted soft kisses. "You like?"

"I like."

A few swirls of my tongue on his nipples got me all hot and bothered. "Your turn."

He moaned. "Do I have to?"

"Yes. It's your punishment."

We had fun that night and many more nights before his heart gave out.

The last words my darling said to me were, "I love you." The next morning I woke up. Jim didn't.

The word funeral drummed in my ears. Frantic phone calls, Cindy rushing home from New York with her fiancée, Len. Arrangements to make. Rachel took over with catering for a wake. Open or closed casket? Open at peace with favorite pictures tucked around my beloved. Buster's old ball thrown many times also placed among his favorite things to take on his next journey. And cremation as we'd decided, ashes to be strewn in the stream below the falls beyond River's Edge in a private ceremony with Cindy.

Following a trail to the stream about five miles north of town, Cindy led the way carrying the urn with Jim's ashes with me clinging to every branch in fear of falling. We looked at each other, at the urn and at the stream filled with rushing water over rocks large and small. "It's time, Mom." She opened the top and together we poured what was left of our sweet man in a place he loved. "He's in heaven, Mom. Above and now right here." She touched her heart. We didn't cry. So many tears had been shed since he left us. I felt hollow inside. My partner in business and life was gone. Nothing left for me to do. Excitement and challenge each day brought because of our teamwork had ended. I looked at a blank slate and didn't know how to fill it.

Showing homes to prospective buyer's needed an experienced person so I appointed Jim's long time associate, Claudia Wilcox, the manager of Trumbull Realtor. Caressing every piece of furniture he ever touched in our home became a habit. Both tears and fingerprints left a trail. One day Rachel sat me down in the kitchen.

"Grace, the furniture is cleaned with lemon polish and it's high time you stopped leaving your mark on everything. I'm too old to be wiping up after you, dear girl." She lifted my chin. "You're wasting away to nothing and we both know Jim wouldn't want you to grieve your big heart out. Either go to counseling or get your ass back to work hard and you'll be better."

"Ass?"

"You heard me, young lady."

Time to pull my act together. Someone once said if you act happy and stay busy, soon you'll be happy and successful. I gave it a shot.

The Pet Emporium needed an extension to accommodate demands from customers. Jim had taken photos of the old building and the restoration when we formed our partnership. I loved the sound of hammers and saws, give and take of the crew as they worked a magical transformation. When the carpenters finished the big project, I had a photographer combine the three stages of growth representing our dream. On a glorious spring day my staff and I had an open house to honor our customers.

First we had the two red fire engines at the head of a parade followed by a float with our dog clients, big and small, all dependable obedience trained. Experienced handlers from all over requested a chance to be part of the day and after vetting them, no one was turned down. The high school marching band came next in full blue and white regalia, baton twirlers, cheerleaders and acrobats in order. New York City papers covered the story as well as local news.

I recalled our opening years before with me at nineteen, pregnant giving away a box of dog treats with a coupon for each appointment. Jim in the background, smiling his approval.

This time we gave dog tags away with each appointment. A stamping machine paid for itself in one day. A light buffet catered by Mimi's Diner and watched over by her number one and two waiters kept the place hopping. Petra and Mike, my faithful groomers for years need more help and I'd hired two more young people with experience and a bookkeeper/receptionist to keep track of business. As for me, I smiled a lot, greeted new and old customers like nothing had changed. Deep inside, I changed. For better, in spite of myself.

Chapter Twelve
I'm Fifty-Four. How did that happen?

"Mother, when did your menopause end?"

Warning bells sounded in my head when daughter, Cindy called me Mother. She turned a two syllable word into three with accent on the first. "Honey, that's an odd question to ask but the answer is I haven't started menopause."

"You mean you still get your uh, cycle?"

"Well, if you really must know, yes. I'm only fifty four and."

"Meet us at River's Edge Steak House in half an hour."

Bossy only child, I thought and hurried to change from my working smock as owner of the Pet Grooming Emporium on Main Street in upstate New York, to wear something more appropriate to the fanciest restaurant for miles around. Fortunately Cats day finished early, my end of the day assistant Kathy had swept the floors clean and left.

Alone, I surveyed the few outfits hanging in the closet and wrinkled my nose. Time to lose ten or twenty pounds and buy fresh, more up-to-date clothes. For what? For yourself, you dope. Take pride in all you've accomplished. Oh yeah. The me I've forgotten about.

Showered and dressed in a loose blue sweater and long flowered skirt, I looked in the full length mirror. What stared back was an aging hippie sans beads and flowers in my hair.

Searching through my jewelry box, I found the gold locket on a thin chain given to me by my first love. College--1960. I hooked the gold chain around my neck.

I drove the fifteen miles through sleepy rush hour traffic in River's Edge, waving to customers if they honked or yelled, "Hey." Small towns where life is simple. My daughter lives further south closer to New York City where she and her husband, Len, commute to work each day. Both lawyers, childless after years of fertility treatments. Hmm. Can this sudden interest in my menopause be linked to the personal question about me?

I pulled into the parking lot of the rustic lodge to be greeted by the owner himself, Larry Owens and his current hunting dog, Buddy Boy, a Golden Retriever I groomed often. I had a fleeting thought about the time Larry asked if I'd uh, consider grooming him once in a while. We remained friends because I didn't smack the married man upside his attractive head. I'd never forget the evening when I'd stumbled into River's Edge, met my best new friend, married that wonderful man, Jim Trumbull, who introduced me to Larry. And now sadly, my precious Jim had passed on after guiding me through years of love, business and the wonder of motherhood.

A handsome devil, actually the master and his dog, one kissed my chubby cheek, the other slobbered lavish wetness on my open palm. Nice to be welcomed on a summer night after all the meowing through the day.

"Cindy and Len are waiting for you. We seated them outside with a terrific view of the falls and the river."

"Thanks, Larry. I know the way."

He took my arm anyway and escorted me up the old wooden steps, through the beamed ceiling rooms and gleaming planked walls through the glass doors at the rear. I heard the rush of water hitting rocks on the plunge down the mountain and falling into the river bed before I recognized Cindy's voice.

"Mother, we're here." Len stood and pulled back a chair for me to sit at a cozy round table for three.

A shrimp cocktail, my favorite, waited for me with a small silver two pronged fork and two lemon slices. Also a crystal glass of Chardonnay sat begging my lips to take a sip. I had a distinct feeling this pre-order was a haste not to waste a moment of precious time.

Am I this predictable, I wondered recalling Jim saying that to me during a moment of romance. Like same old Mom. "What's the rush, kids? Maybe I choose not to have shrimp cocktail tonight."

"Oh, Mom, you always, always begin with this appetizer. Right, Len?"

He nodded and lifted his wine glass. "A toast to the three of us." And for some reason soon to become apparent to me, Len cleared his throat. "As you know, we've been going through fertility treatments for five years now and finally Dr. Ingersol suggested we either consider adoption or."

Cindy cut in. "He also suggested surrogacy and I," she cast a steady look at her husband, "we want to ask you, because we trust you, dear Mom, to be our surrogate."

I choked on a shrimp and gulped down the Chardonnay. "Surrogate as in having your baby?" Was the pounding I heard the sound of the nearby falls or an imminent heart attack? "Do I have to uh, sleep with Len?"

They laughed. I held my breath. "No. It's done by insemination. Dr. Ingersol will explain everything. And I have two frozen eggs we'll use in addition to um, well. Just say yes and it will work out."

Their eager young faces looked at me, the dependable mom who never said no. Automatically I touched the gold locket. I never said no to him either and here I sat some thirty plus years later with our daughter asking please. Big sacrifice for me to possibly carry a baby so my daughter would have a child of her own. Could I do it? Yes. For her, anything. Would I do it was another question.

"You realize this comes as a huge surprise. I'll have to think it over and get back to you Let's have dinner and Cindy, you can tell me about such a procedure step by step since you've been living with infertility issues for several years." I focused my attention on the dearest son-in-law I ever hoped to have. "Len, do you have any calls to make or shows you might watch while we talk?"

"Sure, Mom. A bit of both. It's been a long day. For all of us."

Chapter Thirteen

Len settled down in Jim's home office while Cindy and I sat on the new leather couch purchased recently.

She ran her hands over the buttery yellow soft material. "Nice. I thought you might sell the old house."

I shivered at the thought. "And leave my golden memories behind? No. I feel Jim is here and my pooches keep me company." The rapid click of paws in the hall alerted me to company coming. Princess and Prince wagged short tails in greeting. My sweet miniature poodles followed commands before I allowed them up on our laps.

Cindy ran her hand through Prince's curly hair and scratched behind his ears. "They almost match the couch."

Their apricot color complemented the yellow tone and I had added decorative cushions in brown, yellow and an orange shade. What a decorator. I couldn't dress myself but oh baby, just give me paint and pillows and dogs. "Do you like it?"

"Very much. Now let's get down to business."

I glanced at my daughter. While she appeared calm, I detected hurt in her eyes. I'd held her hand through despair that she wasn't successful in conceiving; a major failure after reaching success in the highly competitive world of lawyers. In my mother's heart I wanted to heal her and give her the baby she coveted if at all possible. Len had gone with her to all the prior fertility treatments and now it was my turn to step up to the plate.

"I've made a chart of what you can expect step by step. It's a tedious process so don't be discouraged. Are you ready, Mom?"

Almost saluting my bossy precise daughter, I said, "Yes, I am."

"Step One. You must meet with a psychologist but with your background, I'm sure you'll pass the test."

I laughed. "Thanks for the faith in little old mom."

"You're not old. Don't say that three letter word again. Step Two. Here's a tricky part. To coordinate our menstrual cycles we'll take birth control pills."

I laughed and couldn't stop at the thought of birth control pills. If only I'd taken them, remembered to take them thirty five years ago, we wouldn't be having this conversation tonight. I clutched her hand and finally caught my breath.

"What's so funny?"

"Oh baby girl. The words birth control cracked me up. Continue please and don't pay attention if I seem like I'm off my rocker every once in a while." I wondered if Jim listened in from heaven and enjoyed a hearty laugh.

"Dr. Ingersol will give you a physical examination. Also an ultrasound and disease screening. an overall health screening. Don't panic, Mom. You'll like the nice doctor."

"Oh my God, Cindy, you sound just like I did when I'd take you to a doctor. "You'll like the nice doctor and then if you're a good girl you'll get a lollipop." This time we both giggled.

"Honey, I hate the sound of this but it's okay. I'm in."

She breathed what sounded like a sigh of relief and consulted her notes.

"Oh, the first day of menstrual cycle and then you begin an evaluation cycle that takes about three weeks."

"Hmm."

"Then, and here comes the big one, we both take birth control pills to coordinate cycles and then a sonogram on you, legal contract signed, Pap smear, treatment cycle and medication to keep from ovulating to receive embryo and," she read faster and faster like a train going downhill. "I take meds to stimulate follicles to release eggs. Three days after eggs are retrieved and fertilized, embryo is transferred to Surrogate. Eleven days later Surrogate is checked for pregnancy. If positive," tears streaked her lovely face smearing eye make-up but who cared, "an ultrasound may be done to determine the sight of implantation and often a heartbeat." We cried together. She finished with the final words, "At four weeks a positive fetal heartbeat may be heard if all goes well."

"How about a glass of wine and some chocolate covered strawberries before our lives are turned upside down?"

"I'll drink to that." Len strolled into the living room and sat down. The dogs jumped into his waiting arms. "We must head home soon, Mom. You girls have a fun time?" He brought a box of tissues from the kitchen and handed it over.

After they left, I walked my little pals to the backyard for a final chance to mark their territory and we all headed upstairs, the house quiet. I decided to roll with the program and not worry what came next. My fate was sealed the moment I'd agreed to be surrogate for them. Sorry? Maybe. In truth, hell yes. So be it. At last I'd give my daughter what she wanted more than anything else in the world.

Rubbing his hands together as if he anticipated the beginning of a great event, Dr. George Ingersol gave me, his new patient, the once over twice. "Welcome Grace Trumbull. I've heard about you for years, way before Cindy became my patient, regarding the Pet Emporium. You are called the dog whisperer."

An aw shucks moment. I managed a smile. "Over rated, Doctor." Gazing at the sci-fi appearance of his office, I recalled Rod Serling's long ago Twilight Zone series on early television. His words, "Being like everybody is the same as being nobody," came back to me. Being a surrogate at my age lifted me out of the everybody class according to the brilliant writer. I like that.

"You've passed the psychologist's examination and today we'll get serious."

Serious? I thought we'd passed serious when I agreed to come here. "Mrs. Wilcox will attend to you before the physical." The trim woman in white took over by handing me a gown. I knew the drill. I'd showered all my parts and dropped my drawers on a neat shelf, folding and hanging as need and steeped out of the private cubicle. Lights, camera, action. Dr. Ingersol returned, armed with enough of an arsenal to explore King Tut's tomb in fantasy land. Eyes shut tight, I prayed for the torture to be over, pass the exam and move to the next phase of what? Oh yes, a sonogram thingy and health inspection. What in the world have I gotten myself into for the sake of my kid and her kid. I focused on petulant poodles, crying Chihuahua's, adorable doodles, sad Salukis and after an interminable time the ordeal ended.

Rubber gloves snapped off, lights turned on and the nice doctor helped me sit. "This is looking very promising, Grace. Schedule another appointment at the front desk."

"I will, George." After all, the nice doctor had just gone where no man had ventured since my sweetheart died. And he didn't take me out for dinner, no drinks, nothing not even a kiss. And now he wanted me to return on command.

He shot me a look, tilted his head and grinned. He got the irony, I thought.

"Please leave a business card at the desk. I have a serious Schnauzer who needs lightning up."

On the way home, I thought about Doctors and patients. They call us by our first names and we're expected to use a title to address them. I studied hard to get be a Certified Pet Groomer. Plus I'm in my mid fifties. I command respect for all my work. So what if I gave up dreams of becoming a veterinarian because I never said no. And my obstetrician, Lorraine Bergen and I became good buddies when I was nineteen and she was forty. So there.

Chapter Fourteen

Three months later

After a dinner filled with joyful tears and lots of glance at my middle making me squirm until I had to say, "Stop," Len asked for privacy to catch up on some calls and we drove back to my home. Cindy squeezed my hand.

"We have a bit of catching up to do, Mom."

Sleep following a busy day of grooming and dinner, I wanted to rest my weary head. "Catching up about what, honey.? So far we're on a successful path with the baby, I'm following doc's orders. So what's to catch up?"

Len parked and in we went to my big old home where Cindy grew up. "Use my office, Len. Mi casa, su casa."

"Thanks, Mom."

Cindy kicked off her heels, sat on the comfortable couch and cleared her throat. "Sit next to me, Mother."

Oh no. Mother, again. Now what?

I needed to sit for what came next.

"You must remember how I always wanted a bunch of relatives and how envious I was of all the kids in my class who had grandparents and cousins and aunts and uncles."

I wanted to cry. Yes. I'd never forgotten how deprived my little girl felt comparing how solitary her life was in comparison to all the other kids she knew. "Yes, I remember and I'll never forget how inadequate I felt at times but you had a wonderful dad and Rachel and dogs. I guess no toys or movies gave you what you needed to fill your heart. I'd stolen that from you by leaving home but Cindy, my parents forced me to leave when I got pregnant. They were ashamed of me and wanted me to give you up for adoption. So I ran away without telling the boy. We had just started dating and made a careless mistake. I certainly didn't want to force him to marry me and ruin his plans. We were only nineteen and he twenty one and both stupid." I took a breath, brushed away tears and held my stomach hoping the baby wouldn't feel my angst.

My precious daughter moved closer and embraced me. "Mom, I know your story, our story, and I've learned to understand. There's something I've never told you and, well, now's the time." Her blue eyes stared right into mine. "I tracked down my grandparents a long time ago when I took classes at law school. One class taught how to find people and I'm a quick learner, you know." I nodded, surprised and taken aback at the revelation. "They'd moved to an assisted living place in Florida because grandpapa had heart trouble and grandma couldn't take care of him alone."

Grandma. Grandpapa. Cindy spoke of the same people, my parents who'd thrown me out at nineteen, pregnant with money my grandfather left his only grandchild for her future. Instead I needed it to take care of a baby with hospital, doctors, shots, clothes, bills and a place to live. There was no end to it. I definitely had to depend on the kindness of strangers many times until that lucky day. Instead of my dream of becoming a veterinarian, I learned to groom animals How fortunate for me, for us to have landed in River's Edge and I found the perfect husband and father for my daughter. Choices. And now I looked at my daughter, a grown woman speaking of the same parents who cast us aside as if we were trash thirty plus years ago or more.

I paced the room. Drank water. Wanted to throw up. "So you're saying you've been in touch with them?"

She flinched. "Well, yes. For a long time."

"You realize they literally threw me out. They were disgusted and embarrassed by my uh, situation. That's what they called the pregnancy, Cindy. A situation. And you embrace them after that?"

"Mother, things were different back then. They're old and ill and sorry. I forgave them." Cindy held out her arms to me. I couldn't resist. I never could say no. That's me. "Open your big heart and remember good times. Think of our baby. We make choices, some good, some not so good. Do you regret having me?"

"Oh honey. Never. We always had each other. And don't you ever forget your father. Jim loved you as if you were his birth daughter."

"I know, Mom. I'll always love, Daddy Jim. But I've wondered forever about my other dad. What's his name, Mom?

She hadn't asked about him before. I pictured his face with high cheek bones and an almost square chin, curly blond hair like Cindy's, blue eyes like Cindy's, long and lean body. Again like Cindy. Even now my heart beat a little faster thinking of him. "His name is Scott Dwyer."

Chapter Fifteen
First Love

At work toward the end of one day, two months pregnant and feeling good I received a call from the nervous owner of a petulant poodle. As if I'm a dog whisperer she knew I could put the dog on a couch and solve her problems.

Taking full advantage of my preoccupation, my late day assistant Kathy in full make-up including extra lashes, whined about an aching back and left early tottering in spiked high heels. No pretending once Kathy opened the passenger door of yet another boyfriend's car. I'd find a replacement and give her notice tomorrow.

The day had passed in a furry flurry of dogs, big and small. Ready to wrap it up and lock the door, I heard the front door open and close. I smelled skunk! I yelled for the customer and the animal to hurry. "No time to waste. You strip, get your dog." I checked out the huge black German Shepherd. "What's his name?"

A deep voice said, "King."

"Tell King to get in the largest tub and you climb in with him. I'll get the tomato juice and together. Oh, just do it fast."

The voice gave a hand command to his pet and the royal dog cleared the edge of the tub and stood. K-9 training, I thought and almost spilled the open can of juice on my clothes. I caught a glimpse of powerful shoulders, a strong muscular frame and a great ass before he crouched next to

King. "I read about a remedy created for skunk deodorizer and tried it. I can whip up another batch in a hurry but for now let's use up the tomato juice because," I paused to open another super size can, "my remedy contains peroxide and we must protect King's eyes. The ingredients are 1 Qt 3% hydrogen peroxide, ¼ cup baking soda, and 1teaspoon of liquid soap. King is large so he'll need a double batch. "

For the next fifteen concentrated minutes, the man and I poured rich red tomato juice over the quiet unmoving dog, working it through his coat After all eight cans were emptied, I told King's handler to come out and command King to STAY for just a bit longer. Turning my head away to give him privacy, I caught a glimpse of him in the mirror. At the same time our eyes met in a shock of recognition.

"Grace Meredith?"

"Guilty as charged. And is it really you, Scott Dwyer?"

"In the flesh." He grabbed a big towel and draped it around his waist. "Grace, you disappeared soon after we, uh, got together. Too much beer and marijuana back then, but I wanted to get to know you. I mean it. It wasn't like a one night thing, for me anyway. And then you were gone from school." He frowned. "I remember you planning to be a veterinarian."

"And of all the dog groomers in all the world, you walked into mine."

"Yeah. You loved Casablanca and you always made fun of yourself. So this is where you ended up."

The timer dinged. The proverbial saved by the bell. "King needs a good rinse right now." More conscious of my weight now that I'd seen Scott's body, I grabbed a big water proof smock and together we sluiced water all over the magnificent dog until the tomato red ran all clear. He shook himself dry, water spraying everywhere in the plastic covered area and then I gave him a sniff test to make sure an all clear skunk seal of approval meant good to go.

After me sneezing a few times, I gave a thumbs up to Scott. He toweled down his dog with gentle care and had me wishing if only. A pipe dream to nowhere.

"So you are with the police force?"

"Yeah. Captain Dwyer, here. K-9 is my specialty. Am I skunk free, too? Just asking since you applied the sniff test to my dog and I thought maybe."

"Maybe what?" Bedraggled, hair wet and straight, make-up gone from a day's work and then the skunk job. All in all, not a pretty sight and certainly not Grace from college days.

He beckoned to me. "Come a little closer, Grace. I won't bite. Promise."

"I bet you say that to all the dog groomers. Wait a minute. Are you married?" I saw a flicker of pain in his eyes. He shook his head. "Divorced, widower?" And I took a step closer.

Scott whispered, "Grace," and I pictured us in the stacks at the library, aflame with burning desire. "Oh, Grace. How long has it been?"

"About thirty six years." I knew because I was a naïve virgin and Cindy came from the wonderful times Scott and I were intimate.

We kissed, tentative at first and the hunger grew until I had no power to stop our awakened need for each other. He pulled back.

"Are you married?"

"I'm a widow.

"Oh. Were you married a long time?"

"Yes. He was a wonderful man, a realtor in town who became my partner in business here." I gestured to the shop.

"I have a small apartment upstairs. Come. Bring your dog and we'll catch up. My pooches are home with my housekeeper tonight. I'll call and ask her to stay a while longer." I hung my plastic smock on a hook to drip dry and walked upstairs. Time to set the record straight. The baby I'm carrying is Scott's grandchild and he doesn't even know he has a daughter. Secrets. They catch up with you, Grace.

To fill the silence, I babbled . "Coffee, tea, a drink?" Me, I really wanted to say and bit my tongue.

"Sit."

I sat and so did King. Scott and I burst into laughter. The command was for his dog and I obeyed. How goofy. Heat rushed to every part of my body. I still loved him.

"Fill me in, Grace."

Again we laughed. Fill me in the old expression before making love.

"Okay, you tell me why you ran away in 1960. Was it because you were pregnant and afraid to tell me?" I nodded. "Afraid our futures would be ruined because of a baby or what?"

"My parents disowned me and I," tears held in check for years trickled down, "and I feared you'd feel the same way so I ran."

"And we lost precious time, Grace but there's no going back. So you found your way to River's Edge eventually and began your grooming business and you married and made a good life here."

"Yes." He wiped away my tears. "And you? You married, became a police officer and now you're a widower." He nodded.

"Tell me about our child. What's his or her name, show me pictures, tell me everything."

"You don't have children?" Again I caught a fleeting flicker of pain.

He shook his head. "First our child."

"Please don't hate me for what I did. Running away and all."

"I promise. Life's too short and getting shorter by the minute."

"Her name is Cindy Scooter Trumbull."

"Scooter? Everyone called me Scooter."

I reached for the ever present album of my, our daughter. We poured over pictures from infancy through college graduation to winning her first law case. "She looks like me."

"Yes, she does. Blue eyes and curly blond hair where mine is straight." I touched my hair and face. "I'm a mess. Hair all straggly, no make-up and chubby. I must smell like dog after all the pets and then King's skunk attack."

King lifted his great head with straight pointed ears at the mention of his name. Scott gave him a biscuit and pointed to the floor. His magnificent dog chewed and settled down again.

Scott leaned over and sniffed my skin. "You're perfect."

I ran trembling fingers through his thick graying hair and inhaled his scent, no tomato juice or skunk remaining. Flustered I rose.

"Scott, I think we should have dinner and catch up before taking this to the next level."

He sighed. I saw disappointment and regret in his eyes. "You're right this time, Grace. But know this," he pulled me close, "this time we're not going to lose each other. No way." The steel in his voice rang with authority. God, I loved him then and still love him.

"Dinner here after I shower. You relax with King. Watch a movie, the news, read a book. Oh, keep yourself busy until I come out."

He laughed, King barked and I locked the bedroom and bathroom doors, hands shaking. Get hold of yourself, Grace. He won't like a pregnant old lady. After showering and drying my hair, I dressed in a loose outfit Cindy bought me. Ralph Lauren blue jean wide pants with a patterned shirt. I tied a silk scarf around my neck and thought the new me looked just fine.

"Your turn, Scott."

I found him thumbing through one of Cindy's albums again. This one had wedding pictures of me in a white lace tent dress and Jim and our friends laughing. He gazed up at me. "You're more beautiful now, Grace. Sit next to me and give me a timeline. Please. I want to know what became of you. Of us."

So I sat next to him. He sniffed my skin as if he wanted to inhale all of me. I didn't move for fear he'd notice my rounded shape and he turned pages. "After I wrote the stupid goodbye letter to you, the tenth draft, I drove all the way up to Buffalo to tell my parents what happened thinking they'd take care of me."

"Obviously they didn't."

"Right. Mother wanted me to have an abortion or give the baby away so I turned around and drove not knowing where to go until I stopped and met a nice Doctor who confirmed the pregnancy and gave me pre natal vitamins and I drove on until another good person gave me directions to River's Edge and."

"You met a lot of kind people. On the other hand, a girl alone, terrible things can happen."

"They didn't. I drove into town, went to a realtor and met Jim, married him," I pointed to the goofy picture and told him about how the Pet Emporium became a partnership venture, "and Scott, Jim was forty when we married and happy to be Cindy's father. I was this lost kid trying to find my way and I did. With his support and authority in town. We had a good life."

I rose, grabbed his hand and pushed him toward the shower. "Clean up while I make dinner. Then I want to know all about you."

The fridge didn't offer a great selection so I called my favorite take out and by the time Scott came out smelling just the way I did, the doorbell rang. "Tucci's Italian here to serve you, Grace." King stood on the alert. I called for Scott. A K-9 dog listens only to his handler. Scott gave a command and King obeyed rewarded with a biscuit while I paid Georgio, my special delivery boy. "Thanks for good fast service."

"No cooking here?"

"No food here. Not today. Set the table for a feast." I unwrapped a quarter of a chicken breast with mushrooms and spinach for me and two whopping lasagna slices for Scott with a salad for two complete with olives, hearts of Romaine, tomato slices, slivers of red onion, and crisp croutons. Dressing on the side.

I lit two candles and we sat opposite each other. I wanted to jump his bones before and after dinner. "Bon appétit." Eating slowly, I watched Scott wondering what his life had been the past thirty five years and knew I had to wait 'til after dinner.

"This is delicious, Grace. Do you order in often?"

"If you're asking do I entertain gentlemen callers up her, the answer is no. Not ever. Sometimes when my staff and I are too pressured to stop for lunch, we'll call and Marconi's delivers. It's a family owned business like many in River's Edge. Where do you live?"

He rolled his shoulders to relax them, a motion I recalled from the few months we were together.. "Rockland County. Pearl River. It's a big town, the largest enclave of Irish in the States." He grinned. "The St. Patrick's Day parade is something to behold."

We finished dinner; he fed King and walked him while I wondered what to do when they returned. The question was answered when they came up the stairs and King lay down. Scott and I sat on the couch and swapped stories about past years.

"What brought you up to this neck of northern New York?"

He stretched his long legs, ankles crossed and half smiled showing a dimple in his cheek. "I have time off and decided to check out the place where there are waterfalls and streams I've heard about. Also I wanted a place where King could roam free for a while." He shook his head, a blond lock of hair falling across his forehead. "Bad mistake. That's where King met skunk and skunk won." Suddenly he pulled me in his arms and we kissed. Years peeled away but this time I could say no.

"No, Scott. Not yet. Tell me more. Tell me everything and I'll tell you so we can fill in the blanks."

"Okay, but stay close or I'll come after you again." Oh how I wanted to. "And if King hadn't lost the battle today, I never would have found you. Was it a chance encounter? I don't think so, Grace. Meant to be is more like it." Silently I agreed. "1960. You broke my heart by disappearing and I graduated without knowing where you'd gone or why. Everyone partied hard so I made an attempt to join my buddies, drank too much and staggered back to the dorm, packed up and went home to my folks. I did get your parents phone number in Buffalo. You father seemed bewildered about your whereabouts and your mother hung up."

"A far cry from the house with the picket fence and lots of relatives."

Another kiss. "You remember. I didn't know where else to look. If I'd been a cop back then, I'd have put out an APB and found you hiding in plain sight."

He came close, I thought, but no cigar and here we were, no longer kids, in our fifties. Between the two of us, we'd racked up a lot of mileage.

"Cuddle up. I'll reveal all if you will."

"Not a good idea, Scott."

"Hmm. Okay, I'll peel off a layer first and then it's your turn. How's that for a plan?" He nudged me in the ribs just missing my expanding middle. "Like, uh, peeling an onion."

"Or strip poker."

"Even better." His eyes sparkled with enthusiasm just like in the old days.

"I agree on my terms. We have thirty five years to cover. You give me five first."

"One kiss before?"

"No way." I scooted across to the end of the couch and settled in, a pillow across my middle.

"Down, boy." I knew it wasn't King he spoke to. The magnificent animal snored on a rug next to the door.

He appeared to search in some distant place before beginning and then the words poured out. "After graduation, I went to Yale Law planning on law toward an FBI future like so many feds. Finally I decided on John Jay University in NYC for all studies connected with law enforcement. It was a new school, very exciting and I fit in and began to make choices."

"Choices?"

"Yeah. Which direction to take and then," he paused and his enthusiastic expression changed, "I met Pamela Cartwright. And what attracted me to Pam, you might ask?" I shrugged as if I didn't have a clue and I didn't. "She was petite, like you, with silky dark brown hair, like yours. That's where the resemblance ended. We married. Busy with studies and long hours, I didn't realize she drank. A lot. Vodka. And only stopped when she got pregnant. Scott Junior was two months old in a car bed in the back seat of our two-door Ford when she drove to the store one night." His sad blue eyes looked across the couch, across the years, to find mine. One swift move brought me to his side.

"Driving home I passed an accident. Like all the other stupid drivers, I slowed. The car was a dark blue Ford like the one Pam drove. Something inside me said to pull over. A cop waved me along and then he recognized me and came over. I asked him what happened.

"Oh Geez," he said. "Nasty and tragic. This lady slammed into a truck doing seventy miles an hour. She's dead and so,"

Scott choked on tears, "and so is the baby. They were thrown from the car on impact." My long lost love sat quiet and finished. "I knew without looking I'd lost my baby boy and my sick wife."

We held each other for a long time. Down Main Street the town clock chimed ten; birds roosting there scattered in a flapping of wings. Life went on as if nothing had happened in the apartment above the Pet Emporium. After a while I caressed his face and placed his hand on my belly. "Here's some interesting news for you."

He did that familiar tilt of his head so dear to me. "After my first five years of revelation to you, I hope it's an improvement."

"Our daughter, Cindy Scooter Adler, has had infertility problems for a long time and she and her husband Len, you'll love them both, have asked me to be surrogate for their baby."

He frowned. "I don't understand."

"In simple words, I'm going to carry their baby for them."

"What?"

"Yes. And right now I'm two months pregnant with your grandchild."

"Oh. Oh. Oh." His hand caressed my rounding abdomen over and over again. "You mean in here is our grandbaby?"

"Yes. Oh yes." King lifted his great head as if sensing something momentous was going on. The whole idea of sharing the news with Scott curled my socks like the first time he kissed me except I wasn't wearing any socks. I felt like a kid again and didn't say no when gently he led me into the bedroom. Removing my loose sweater turned out to be no problem since I aided and abetted my cop with every move. And how come it ended just like in days of old with me sans clothing and Scott still dressed?

"Well what do we have here?"

At least I smelled good, we both used the same body wash an hour before. Naked I certainly wasn't the skinny virgin when he first saw me sans clothing. I made a feeble attempt to cover up.

"Hey, it's just me, Grace, plus thirty five years of wear and tear. What you see is what you get. No returns this time. You are a fragile orchid, my love. I'll never let you go."

"Good. Fragile, huh? No bungee jumping or bouncing on a trampoline this time around?"

"Nope."

With sweet may I do this? and how about that? Scott and I made it through to the grand finale of love making without damage. Holding hands and catching our respective breaths afterward, Scott asked me to marry him.

"You want to make an honest woman of me, do you?"

"It's about time, don't you think?"

"I think. Tomorrow I'll call our daughter so you can meet her before the wedding."

Chapter Sixteen

Saturday, we cleaned up and trudged downstairs before the staff arrived. Scott crossed the street to pick up breakfast I'd ordered at Mimi's Diner. After he left to return, she called. "You have a new boyfriend, Grace? He's adorable."

"He's slightly used, Mimi. We met in college and got reacquainted last night. By chance."

"Tell me more."

"Not now but Mimi, here's a head's up, he's going to be around from now on." I hung up.

I smelled pancakes the minute he walked in the door. King was out in back on the dog walk so we dined, laughing over nothing. He paced the Emporium waiting for me to call Cindy.

"Honey, are you and Len busy this morning? I have something important to discuss with you. Maybe around noon?"

"Oh Mom, are you okay? Nothing is wrong with the baby, right?"

"Not to worry. I'm fine. Are you free at noon or later today?"

"Just a sec, I'll ask Len." She returned a few minutes later. "Noon is the best time for us. See you then." I heard panic in her voice. My girl. Always in a rush to fix whatever might be going wrong. This time she was in for a big surprise. I chuckled and reached for a smock. Petra and Mike showed up with Johnny and Marge close behind. Customers were already pulling into parking spaces.

I introduced Scott to everyone and noticed the women giving him sideways glances. Definitely a hunk, my guy.

"What can I do to help?

"First take care of King. Then when he's settled down come watch the operation here. We're very organized and we keep the flow of pets moving along with efficiency and a lot of love. If there's a special needs dog, I take over and have a chat with the animal."

"You talk to them to heal them?"

"Yes. It's a gift. I don't know where it came from and I don't question it but they improve. Usually it's personality."

"Hmm." He kissed me as if it were an everyday occurrence and went off to care for King.

The morning passed quickly. I felt Scott's presence behind me as he watched and soon, out of the corner of my eye, I saw him roll up his sleeves and join in whenever someone needed a helping hand.

The BMW pulled up in front and Cindy flew out of the car to enter my shop. She looked around to find me washing my hands. "You're all right!"

"I said I was fine, honey. Bring Len in."

Len raced in and hugged me. "Thank God you're okay, Mom."

"Kids, there's someone I want you to meet. Come upstairs." I beckoned to Scott. His face turned red. I felt his nervousness across the shop. "There's a K-9 trained dog in the apartment. His handler is right behind us. Let him go first." Scott rushed by, entered and spoke to King. We came in.

I spoke rapidly, words pouring out nonstop on one breath."Cindy, this is Scott Dwyer, your birth father. We talked about him the other night and by chance,"

She interrupted me. "I look like you. Oh my God. Len, do you see what I see? It's a miracle. Can I touch you to see if you're real?"

Scott opened his arms and hugged his daughter for the first time. "It is a miracle."

I sat in the old rocking chair and rocked to clear away the anxiety felt before this joyous meeting. Len and I were bystanders for the moment. Bursting with our personal news, I couldn't contain myself anymore. "Scott and I have decided to get married."

"Oh." Cindy's face changed from joy and she frowned. "But what would Dad think?"

"Cindy, he'd want me to be happy again and meeting Scott is a bonus like winning the lottery."

King growled. Scott gave him a command. "So I'm a bonus, huh? Like winning the lottery. You have a way with words, my Grace." He kissed me and turned to the kids. "I'm a lawyer so we begin with a lot in common."

"You are?" Cindy grinned and looked like a little kid. My daughter, so mercurial.

"Yes. I went to Yale thinking FBI and ultimately finished studies at John Jay in NYC. I told your mom all about my past, at least the first five years after we lost touch. She still has to fill me in about her first five. This might take the rest of our lives. Meanwhile, we're having a baby and I'll be with her every step of the way." He tweaked my nose. "No chocolates, young lady. The best healthy food and afterward, we splurge."

"And you're in law enforcement now?" Len jumped in, his intelligent eyes sparkling.

"I'm ready to retire. I'm an officer in the K-9 Corp, narcotic and criminal detection. King is my partner." King barked his approval.

While we lunched at Mimi's in my favorite booth in a far corner, I tackled yet another grilled chicken breast, salad with squeezed lemon for taste. My family made plans for me as if I had no choice in the matter. At this point, I didn't care. Scott and I would marry fast before I'd begin to waddle; he'd accompany me to the nice doctor. Funny how life changed so quickly. Just because a skunk had his way with King. And no longer would Doctor Ingersol be the only man familiar with my private parts. I have Scott. My main man.

"What's so amusing, Grace? Is there something in the salad I should know about?"

"Just stuff. Life." I leaned over to kiss him and share my lemon flavored tongue.

"Not in front of the children, dear."

"They better get married fast. Mom's getting nutsy, Len."

"I can see that."

Chapter Seventeen

Scott's family had lined up on a long covered porch. Like a Norman Rockwell painting, I thought. The white picket fence he'd described when we met in 1960 still there but what a spread of land to encompass. My BMOC came from not so modest a background. Smiles and waves came from all sizes of relatives. At last Cindy and I had it all.

I wanted a simple ceremony. Scott agreed and said his mother had a plan. "Not to worry, honey," he said. "Buy a pretty dress," he said. "Just some friends and family," he said.

"Tell your mom. No gifts. Make a donation for rescue shelters. Um. Just write a check or leave cash and I'll make sure the money goes where it's needed. And I'll send a receipt. We don't need a toaster."

So I bought a wide skirted print summer dress guaranteed to camouflage my middle and white three inch heels and a big floppy straw hat. Perfect for a second hand bride. Scott intended to wear his uniform one last time.

"Are there any more guests coming?" I clutched Scott's hand before all the blond curly headed people who looked a lot like him surged toward us.

"Not to worry, sweetheart. Just a few. Mom had a plan and today's the day you're mine."

His words stayed with me as we were swamped with hugs and kisses. "You've finally found each other. It's a miracle, isn't it, Dad." Lydia, my mother-in-law beamed.

Scott's dad peered over his glasses. "Yes, dear."

I said, "Good answer." All the kids laughed

An hour later I was not prepared for the arrival of fellow officers from Scott's unit, my gang from the Emporium, Mimi from the Diner, and colleagues from Trumbull Realtors.

Cindy stood next to a very old couple; a man in a wheelchair and an elderly woman obviously dressed with care. She waved for me to come over as soon as I could. Scott guided me, made introductions. Lots of handshakes and kisses. Me careful to watch out for too close enthusiastic hugging with Scott in protective mode.

As I approached Cindy and the old folks, my fists clenched. Mother and father withered with age come to. To what? Bizarre, I thought. A Kafka scene of horror on my wedding day. Then I recalled Cindy's story of how she tracked them down years ago and how terrible they felt about the way they treated me. Relax. Calm down. Forgive and let go. A baby is coming and you have Scott.

After taking a deep breath, I greeted my parents, touched their trembling hands and thanked them for coming. Cindy's smile rewarded my generosity of the moment. I never claimed to be saintly. Just older and wiser like our vows.

"They're going to stay long enough to see the ceremony and afterward they'll fly back to Florida. I hope you don't mind, Mom."

I never could resist my daughter. She wanted family and now her dreams were coming true. "It's fine, honey. I have to ask, do I look all right? Scott didn't tell me his mother wanted him to have a big wedding. He said I should buy a summer dress so I did."

She hugged me the way I'd always done to her through the years. "You are the cutest bride, Mom."

Hmm. Cute? At my age. Oh well. Today anything goes.

With a light breeze blowing and the scent of honeysuckle all around, we walked down a makeshift aisle covered by a red carpet toward the Justice of the Peace. A four piece band played "I Can't Stop Lovin' You," our favorite song from 1960. He had the power to pronounce us husband and wife. We had our vows spoken together. "We lost and finally found each other thirty five years later. Fate stepped in and here we are a bit wiser, definitely older, and ready to last forever. That's us. Scott and Grace."

Cheers erupted when we kissed. I didn't hear anyone whisper, "Oh look, she's pregnant." So far so good.

The Dwyer clan spared no expense with an elaborate wedding feast. Striped umbrellas and white table cloths gave the huge yard a festive appearance. Waiters carried trays and offered succulent snacks before the carving began. A chef complete with hat and sparkling white jacket stepped out with a fanfare and dinner was officially served as the sky turned pink to blend with blue and soft billowing clouds made their way across the sky. The band hit Twist and Shout, friends danced and I watched, stirring a few shrimp around my plate. I longed to dance and waited for slower music. We waved off the first dance for bride and groom tradition. Scott whispered. "Are you all right, my wife?"

"Yes. I just didn't expect such a fuss. Um. It's such an extravagant affair."

"Grace, my family has waited for years to see me happy. When I told them I'd found you and we were going to get married right away, they insisted on..." he gestured to the lights, umbrellas, waiters, everything, "I couldn't turn them down. So let's enjoy every moment. You have a big family now, my Grace. Loner no more. And they don't know about our Cindy and our grandbaby." His hand slipped under my dress. I stopped him before anyone noticed.

"Down, boy." We laughed. "Let's slow dance in a little while. We also have to mingle. Not my favorite thing." I noticed Cindy and Len were like politicians doing a meet and greet with poise.

He stood to greet friends from his unit. And took a ribbing over the old guy getting married. I chimed in, "Who said old? You'll have to arm wrestle me for that comment." I made a muscle showing strength from years of lifting dogs and grooming.

"My wife, men. Don't cross Grace Dwyer. She's tough." He kissed the top of my head.

One of the guys said, "What about King? How's he acclimating to the change in venue."

"Grace has King eating out of her hand. I said she's tough and smart. In River's Edge they call her the dog whisperer."

I smacked my husband on the shoulder. "Enough, sweetheart." Pointing to the bar, "I said, "Men, if you're looking around, I do believe you might find some single women over there." They sauntered away toward greener pastures.

Scott pulled me into a full body, gentle embrace complete with a hot kiss leaving me breathless. The gathering clanked cutlery against glasses wanting more. We danced then, no fast moves or turns, just ballroom. "Nice." I snuggled under his chin. "So nice."

Am I being so careful because of the baby and my age? Yes. At fifty-four I can't bop around like a teen. Sorry, old girl.

After thanking Scott's parents, so strong and healthy in their seventies, and waving goodbye and see you soon, we drove home to River's Edge where we'd decided to live in my old home in the woods. After much discussion and taking real estate values into account, why move when we might renovate to our own taste? A sensible idea and we needed a playroom for Junior and our growing canine family. King hadn't met my mini poodles so there were adjustments to be made. We talked all the way home 'til we reached the Emporium where my friend, Annie, a trained handler, stayed in my apartment with King.

They were out in the yard where Annie threw a ball and King raced and caught it every time. We watched through the window and then joined them. King stopped. Scott used his high pitched voice to command King to come. He galloped to his master, his best pal, Scott. Then he came to me and offered his big paw as if to shake in greeting. I almost cried. Our dog. I stroked his big head way back to his tail over and over, deep into the fur to let know I love him.

"How did he do, Annie? Was he much trouble?"

"No. We have a thing going. He ate well and slept well. It was only overnight, Scott. But I'd do it again anytime. He's a good boy."

"Tell that to drug dealers he's helped bring in over the years. Anyway, thanks. How much do we owe you?"

She shook her head. "Grace has been very generous to me through the years. I'm happy to return her kindness. Hey Grace, when's the baby due?"

Caught! "How do you know?"

"Geez, Grace. Everyone in town knows. I'm a mom. I knew right away. Just something about a preggers. Well, God Bless and good luck. It's not easy when you're uh, how old?"

"Annie, get out before I spank you and you know I'm tough enough to do just that. Thanks for taking care of King and hush about me, you hear!" The door closed. Annie's laughter carried in the still night air.

"Scott, our secret is out!"

"No, honey. Forget about it. One day at a time. Now I'll get King's bed and food, pack my bag and we'll move into our new home. Tomorrow I go with you to the doctor and tell him not to peek."

Oh baby. I'm in for a fun filled time. A husband who doesn't want the doctor to look at my privates, is he kidding or what? The whole town knows I'm with child, and NO CHOCOLATE. I laughed all the way home.

Laughing no more when King met my miniature poodles, Prince and Princess. They came up to the first joint in his hind quarter. "I'll handle this." Scott assured me he had control of a delicate situation. My dogs, their domain. King, the interloper. A huge scary interloper.

The command to stay didn't help for long when my little guys sniffed all around the mountainous creature. King joined in the sniffing party, seemed to approve of the small critters at his feet and gave a lick that knocked Princess over. A game began; a lick then a roll over and bounce back of small acrobatic poodles.

We stepped back and laughed ready to intercede in case of danger. Finally my man walked, watered, and fed them all and spread King's bed out near the front door Scott and I went up the stairs to honeymoon, carefully.

Chapter Eighteen

Dr. Ingersol looked up perplexed. "I hear two heart beats. One must have been hiding behind the other. This is not good news for a surrogate your age."

"What?" Scott and I said at the same time."You mean twins are in there?"

"Yes. And Grace, you must make a decision to um, only have one."

Scott almost grabbed the nice doctor by the throat. "You mean kill one baby?"

"Mr. Dwyer, I realize you're intense about this grandchild but it's wiser for Grace to carry one. For her health and for the baby. Think about it. I'll be right back." The doctor ran for his life as far I could tell.

"Calm down honey. We'll research the problem and make a rational decision. Personally for a healthy specimen like me, I'm not in favor of selective termination. It sounds so, uh Nazi like."

"No, Grace, it's for health reasons when necessary. We'll listen to Doctor Ingersol and get Cindy and Len over for a consultation. If this means you have to have bed rest, take it easy, off your feet, it's only for a few more months. Let's get him back here and listen. I'm sorry I went ballistic."

The doctor returned. I had dressed and we sat at in his office and tried to appear calm. As if we dropped in for tea.

Scott apologized for flying off the handle. The doctor accepted. All very civilized. "Please explain possibilities and consequences so we can make a decision, Dr. Ingersol."

After clearing his throat, the doctor said, "There's a risk to you, Grace because of your age. Carrying twins is not easy at any age. If you do carry both of them, you may very well require bed rest, absolutely no sexual activity, and most likely an early delivery. Pregnancy is difficult at best. Your situation doubles the precariousness of the situation. And you must consult with your daughter and her husband before a final decision. That said," he folded his hands, "you are in remarkable good health. That's a plus." He rose. Our little talk had ended.

We rode down in the elevator holding hands. "Time for a family Pow Wow. Carry me to the car, big guy."

A little humor goes a long way. At home, I called Cindy. "Hi honey, we just got back from the doctor."

"And what did he say. How are you?"

"We've got double trouble and need you and Len to come over for a conference."

"Double?" She shrieked. "Twins? We'll be there in an hour." She hung up.

Meanwhile, Scott fed the dogs that got along as if they were all the same size, and booted up the computer. Time to check on older surrogates who delivered twins. He muttered singles, singles, singles, and suddenly Eureka as if he'd discovered fire. "I've got a hit on one woman from Australia who carried for her son's wife and delivered twins a year ago. All of them are healthy. And here's another in New Zealand who successfully had twins at fifty three. So far it's good, Grace."

I moaned. "Find someone in New York so I can talk to her." I whined. "I'm hungry."

"Me too. Warm up the lasagna from last night and I'll broil salmon for you with risotto rice." I knew right away my husband would not pamper me unless he felt it absolutely necessary.

By the time the kids arrived, we were settled down and ready to discuss a complex situation.

Cindy and Len, on the other hand, arrived rattled and fearful.

"What have we gotten you into, Mom?" Cindy cried. Scott gave her a command worthy of a K-9 hostage situation.

"Let's approach this rationally or Grace and I will decide without your histrionics." She stopped the floodgate of tears. "We are against selective termination and feel the best solution, since your mother is in good health for any age, is for her to allow her assistants to do the heavy lifting at The Emporium. She can continue with her dog whisperer amazing talents and stay off her feet as needed. As the babies grow, I'll assume more work. Already I've learned some grooming techniques and will continue. We'll have full time help at home and Dr. Ingersol will keep a close watch on her progress."

He held me in his arms as if that would protect me for the months to come. Maybe it would all work out, I thought. Wishful thinking taken to a new level.

Scott said, "You're up."

They appeared to be stunned as they glanced at each other and stared at us. We had made the decision before they arrived. Len began. "The most important factor is Mom's health. We've prayed for a baby for five years and suddenly it's complicated. We don't want to lose one."

"Or the other." Cindy sat on the floor and touched our hands. "Let's do what you've said, Dad and pray for the best." After a long silence, she stood and made chamomile tea. "Any chocolate chip cookies around here, Mom?"

"No caffeine until after the births. There are some cookies in the pantry. Enough for three. I'll have some raisins. Oh yummy."

I shut my ears to their talk about older surrogates in far off lands who had twins. Enough already. Go home and leave me alone with a good book and our dogs. No sex and no chocolate. Five months to go and who's counting. What a life.

Chapter Nineteen

Singing "The falling leaves drift by my window. . ." was an optimistic way to begin the day. I pictured Doris Day singing the song, hitting every note, me a teenager straining for the high notes and giving up. I switched to "And the days dwindle down to a precious few," feeling the bump, kicks, and roll of kids one and two responding to the music. I patted my belly and hoped they'd calm down.

"Scott, will you still love me with a scar on my belly after the C section?"

"No." He came close to me and lifted my once baggy tee shirt, now stretched to capacity. Warm strong hands spread across to measure the width and girth of me. Fingers did a stealthy march to the dark moist of me. "I want to love you like I've never loved you before. Right now."

"Oh, Scooter. Lie down and let me satisfy you until this is over. It won't be much longer. Maybe a month. Yes. One more month and they'll be cooked. A C section is over without the pain and hours of labor."

After the loving of my good man, we lay together eyes closed until I felt a sharp kick way down low. I didn't like the feeling at all. "Scott, call the Doctor and get me to the hospital right now."

He made the call, carried me out the door and we were off. Dr. Ingersol and his best staff were there waiting as Scott pushed the wheelchair into the emergency room. After close examination, the good doctor looked grim. "Let's do a section right now. She's going into labor."

"Doctor, is there a way to stop labor and give the babies a chance to stay where they are for a little longer?"

Dr. Ingersol looked at my husband for one long moment as if who was this moron to challenge my judgment. Then a different expression crossed his face. "There is an old fashioned method we can try. It's worth a chance for maybe a half day." Briskly he ordered a drip for me, something saline, I couldn't make out what he said.

Scott squeezed my hand. The process began. Throughout the day, I dozed, and Scott, ever vigilant, stayed at my side. The doctor came in and smiled after listening to my insides. "Ah. Very good. Thanks, Mr. Dwyer. Have you had previous experience?"

"Yes. As an officer in the K-9 Corp for many years, you come across many situations and I remembered a woman we found going into labor prematurely and one of the cops in my unit called a medic who did exactly what you just accomplished. And not in the cleanest environment."

I heard what sounded like a mutual sigh of relief. "We'll keep Grace here for a few days to monitor her. After this scare, if she can hang in for a month, we're home free."

"Bite your tongue, Doc. We'll do the best we can."

Don't alarm the kids became our motto. Whenever Cindy called, like five times a day, Scott said I was fine. Or I answered and chirped, "Cool, not to worry."

Four days later, I went home. We agreed it was a close call. Three weeks more to go. The forecast called for snow. It started with a light dusting. We laughed watching the dogs frolic in the yard we finally fenced in for safety.

"It's gonna be a big one." The jolly weatherman carried on from his warm studio and pointed to an unreadable screen of snow, rain and more across the northern eastern part of the US. At this time we weren't interested in what was going on anywhere else. Scott piled wood inside and set the fire blazing with tight twisted newspaper as kindling. Feet up on an ottoman, I sighed and hoped today was not the day.

Warning came during the height of the storm. Pain radiated across my lower back enough to scare both of us to get moving and fast. Light snowflakes became a blizzard when Scott, once again, phoned the doctor and windshield wipers going like a runaway metronome, drove me to the emergency room. This time Dr. Ingersol rushed us to the fourth floor for delivery. My husband's face pinched with worry. "I love you, Sweetheart. See you and the kids in a few."

This time, full of confidence, I put myself in the nice doctor's hands and used yoga breathing exercises to help relax. I visualized palm trees, a beach with waves lapping at the shore to create my own space and only half listened to preparations and the speed as my doctor worked to take my grandchildren from me and bring them into the world.

A healthy cry from baby one rang out followed by a softer squeal from baby two a few minutes later. "Grace, they look perfect." Dr. Ingersol spoke to me, his voice had a satisfied sound to it. "Your grandson weighed in at four pounds, two ounces and his sister topped the scale at four pounds even. They have curly blond hair like their mother." He leaned over and spoke softly. "I'm so proud of you. For what you've accomplished as my oldest surrogate and the care you've taken to help make this happen."

"Ask Scott to come in and I really need some dark chocolate."

He chuckled. "Your husband's on his way but no chocolate until later. Please." He patted my foot. I wondered why the hell doctors do that. Doctoring 101?

"Did you see our kids?"

Tears ran down his face. "I couldn't be with you for our daughter's birth but here we are with two grandkids. Grace, we'll be the best grandparents ever."

"Honey, I've heard the best thing about being a grandparent is that you don't have to pay for their education and when they visit and go home, you wave bye-bye and the house is quiet again."

We both glanced over at the baskets where the babies slept. Swaddled in blue and pink, little knitted caps on their heads, tiny fists curled, they were delicious. Cindy and Len arrived to go nuts over their newborns. The Palisade Parkway was in progress of being cleared and they had to follow a snowplow most of the way from New York City. They were allowed five minutes to see the twins and after hugs to me, Scott, Cindy and Len went down to the cafeteria. Peace at last. I slept until a nurse came in.

"The room reserved for Mr. and Mrs. Len Adler is ready."

"They might be in the coffee shop. Please page them." I'd forgotten in all the rush they'd stay for a few days to learn how to care for the babies from a special nurse. They had hired someone a while ago and she'd live-in for a few months and probably longer since my daughter was a lawyer. As far as I knew, Cindy had already enrolled them in nursery school, dance, music lessons, and computer classes. And maybe Law School. I'd have to convince her to let them be kids for a long time first.

With that happy thought, I closed my eyes and dreamed of sex and dark chocolate, in that order.

The Beginning. . .Not The End

Housebroken

by

Charmaine Gordon

Dedication

This story is dedicated to my husband, Don, because he knows what's what about humor and love, two ingredients to keep a house from being broken.

I hear his voice in the background saying, "You've housebroken me, my dear wife."

Acknowledgements

To Kimberlee Williams who raised this primitive author by teaching me enough to use my computer fairly well. My friend, because you believed in me, I believe in me. Thank you for everything. Here's to success, good health, and joy.

Chapter 1

Steve and Sally Atwood held their respective breaths and prayed nothing would upset the get-away. Two children out and now, at last, the youngest married and going, going, gone. They waved and watched Johnny and his bride drive down the road and turn the corner in their new Toyota.

"Alone at last." Steve hugged his wife of thirty-five years. "Let our honeymoon begin." And to his surprise when he lifted her chin for a kiss, he discovered tears running down her cheeks. "What's this, honey? I thought you'd be happy."

She sniffled and blotted tears on his shirt. "I am happy, but now," Sally raised her arms and walked through the hall into the kitchen and through the dining and living rooms, "the house is empty. Once it was filled with children, sweet babies laughing and crawling. . ."

"And crying all night and teenagers asking for the keys to the car and thinking they knew more than we do." He pulled her to him. "Sweetheart, you've forgotten the effort we've put in to raising three kids to be good people and now it's our turn at last. How about champagne to celebrate alone at last and I bought your favorite chocolate covered strawberries? I'll fill the hot tub and we'll relax."

Sally kissed her husband, knew he was right and he'd pushed all the right buttons with decadent drinks and chocolate in the afternoon. She pulled the scrunchy from her hair as she climbed the stairs, and she sucked in her belly, glad she'd done a zillion sit-ups to strengthen her muscles and keep up her shape. The allure of sweets called to her. She'd resisted – so far.

Steve waited 'til she entered the bathroom before popping the cork to pour champagne. Sally did a coy strip tease and carefully stepped into the tub to sit and soak in hot bubbly water. They clinked crystal flutes, made a toast "To us" and breathed in the heady fragrance of lavender. Steve fed strawberries to his wife; they shared each one and, when dessert ended, they had no doubt about the pleasure ahead.

Chapter 2
One month later

"Sally? I'm home."

Steve's voice broke the silence and Sally felt a tinge of annoyance. In the midst of writing an article for the local paper, she needed concentration and all he wanted was sex. Well sex was good, uh, great but she needed a time-out. As a would-be journalist, getting clients, submitting articles, becoming a name turned out to be hard work. And damn social media for taking over to create another challenge. Steve had a solid position with a large corporation as managing sales director of the entire country. He had no idea how hard she worked in an attempt to reach the first rung of the ladder at her age.

"The weather forecast is grim. Big snowstorm coming." He opened the fridge. "We're short on milk, butter, bread, cat food and what did you plan for dinner?"

Dinner, who gives a flying... She called out. "Fluffy died two months ago and already you've forgotten our sweet girl."

She left the office created from Johnny's bedroom the day after he left and hurried downstairs to greet her big bear of a husband. "I'm sorry, sweetheart. I've been in all day writing an article about a new restaurant in town. And this time I not only get paid," she gave him a big wet kiss, "I get a byline because the editor likes the personal angle."

"Mmm. I like your personal angle with or without pay. Sorry about Fluffy. We'll get another pet soon. But we better get over to the store fast."

"Great. I'll get my coat and boots. Oh, I forgot. My boots are shot." Her eyes sparkled, remembering a big sale at Macy's. "How about you do the grocery shopping and I run in for boots. One trip and we accomplish two things before the storm."

He grumbled. "Well, make it fast. I'm a good shopper."

On the way to the new mall in Nanuet where watermelons and boots were available almost side by side in beautiful clean shops, they found a nearby parking space someone just vacated. Snowflakes began to fall from a sky filled with piled high ripe clouds.

"Good thing we traded in the SUV for a sedan. I love this two door BMW."

Sally grinned. "It's perfect for the two of us."

They parted with a kiss. "Hurry. I'll meet you at the car in half an hour tops," Steve said and Sally ran.

On the dot, Sally staggered back, three boxes of boots and shoes packed in a Macy's bag, to find the car with snow piled on at least two inches deep. Snow brush in hand, Steve swept away the windshield and windows. "Squeeze in and let's get going. The ice cream's melting."

"Ice Cream? We weren't going to buy ice cream until we lost weight."

"Yeah but Haagen Daz is on sale."

The Macys' bag fit in the small trunk where groceries should have been. Instead Steve had piled bags of food in back and on the passenger seat. Sally yelped when she sat on cold carrots, lumpy potatoes and heaven knows what.

You gotta have a sense of humor. All this togetherness isn't what it's cracked up to be.

116

Chapter 3
Three months later

"What's for dinner?" Words to make Sally shiver were the first Steve said, returning from a three day business trip.

"Hi honey. I'm so happy to be home with the one I love most in the world. Steve, try saying that when you come home. You'll be rewarded with more than a peck on the cheek."

The sound of his travel bag thumped on the entrance floor. He swept her into his arms, bent her back for a kiss and came close to dropping her. "Oh my back. Geez. I can't make the moves I used to."

"What's better, an ice pack or a heating pad?"

"Ice pack. Do we have any percocet left?"

Sally ran to the closet. She found a bottle with a few still rattling around.

"Water please and the pill. That'll do it. Give me about half an hour to recuperate and then I'm taking my best girl in the world out for dinner. What's your pleasure, sweetheart?"

"Hmm. We haven't had ribs for a long time."

An hour later, with Steve's back pain relieved, off they drove in their new Mercedes to the best rib place in Rockland County, Giovanni's The Place for Ribs.

Over cocktails, they talked about their kids. Sally gave Steve an update.

"Johnny called. I mean Jonathon. Pardon me but that's the way he's chosen to be addressed not just by the law firm and his wife but also by us."

An olive spurted from Steve's mouth. Almost choking, face red, he gulped the martini and ate the olive.

"Are you okay?"

"Sure. There's nothing a martini can't cure."

She raised her wine glass still full of chilled Chardonnay. "Here's to our good health." She sipped and savored the cool taste.

"Remember the night our only boy was born?"

"Who can forget?" Steve chuckled. "Twenty eight years ago, two hundred thousand dollars, at least—to pay for education for a colicky baby we didn't think would amount to much. Jonathon, kiss my royal butt."

"And now some sweet unsuspecting girl married him."

"God love the two of them. You and I are alone, together. Don't order anything else to drink. I have to drive or maybe you're the designated driver."

The waiter brought two plates of baby backs, ramekins with baked beans, a corn bread square and fries. Also two glasses filled with water topped with a slice of lemon. They dug in with the knowledge they'd take some home for lunch the next day.

A walk around the block after dinner seemed like a good idea so Sally and Steve held hands and strolled checking out the neighborhood.

"It's changed since we bought the house here thirty years ago, Steve."

"So have we."

"When we moved in, everyone was young with little kids. Play dates weren't necessary. Kids came to the door. Every day was like a party."

Spring weather in New York had just arrived. Crocus bloomed close to the large houses. Steve burped. "Pardon me. I ate too many ribs." He pointed to the house next door where new neighbors were installing a playground. "Now we have new folks with small kids. Face it, we're the old ones now."

Taking a deep breath, Sally spoke up. "There's something on my mind. Let's sit on the deck. Remember when we called it a porch?"

Steve laughed out loud. "I'll get some Tums and then I'm sure you'll let me know everything that's on your mind just the way we've done for so many good years."

This time, Sally wasn't so sure her husband would be eager to hear her thoughts.

Chapter 4

Sally loosened her belt and sighed, inhaling the fresh night air before bugs and humid weather settled in. She dusted off the reclining lounge chairs and sat with Steve next to her loving the his and her coziness, a couple forever to ride into the sunset together.

"We've out grown this house, my dear. I mean this house is way too big for two."

"What do you mean? It's perfect. I know where everything is. I love our house."

She took his hand. "Steve, I've been thinking about this for a while. Yes, we know where everything is and it's a comfort. But and here comes the big BUT, we've accumulated things we don't need and. . ."

"So give them away. Have a garage sale or give to one of the Veteran's organizations or. . ."

"Calm down. I don't want your blood pressure to go sky high again. I've already thought about that. There's more. Our lovely deck is rotting."

At the nasty word, Steve struggled out of the lounge chair and checked the wood." It's peeling, that's all. A little sanding here and there, some paint and the deck will look good as new."

She shook her head. "I called for a free estimate from a local man called Handy Husband. When he heard how old the deck is without weatherproofing and the new treatments available, he confirmed what I suspected."

"Handy Husband, my ass. Of course the bandit told you the worst, Sally. He wanted to scare you."

She moved on to her next concern. "About the roof. I picked up five shingles from the yard. They were faded and disgusting underneath and came from our roof. It's obvious the roof needs replacing or whatever they do. Taxes are too high and we pay for education and we no longer have kids in school."

Steve's face assumed a thoughtful business-like appearance. "You're hitting me from out of left field but I kind of see your point. So you're suggesting we sell and move where?"

Ah, the sticking point, she thought. "I saw an ad by owner for a corner townhouse in a less expensive town and there's a small cottage for sale by the Hudson River."

He stood knocking over his lounge chair to pace what his wife called the rotting deck. "Moving to a small cottage where we'd live out our lives using candles to light our way? How romantic. You've been reading too many romance novels. A corner townhouse? Neighbors attached? Sally, what's come over you? Did some handsome young realtor sell you a bill of goods? Well, I'm not buying it." He slid the sliders shut with a bang.

That didn't go too well, she thought and returned to her computer determined to search for possibilities in nearby towns. After all went quiet upstairs, she concentrated. Before long a listing appeared and then another. She was weary of cleaning this house with a never ending accumulation of dust and Steve telling her that since the kids were gone, she didn't need maid service. Her days were filled with cleaning, writing articles of interest for the local papers in hopes of jump starting a career for herself. Somehow, Steve's libido had come to life in a big way and she had more than enough sex for a woman of her age.

"Sometimes it takes me three days to wake up in the morning." Sally looked around. Did she just say that? Yes and to the four walls with no one to hear her plea. She laughed 'til tears spilled down her cheeks. Feeling good, she hit print and new listings flew out of the printer. "We'll check them out tomorrow."

Swaggering out of the small office, Sally climbed the stairs to the bedroom where Steve snored. She stripped and slid between the sheets to press close to his warm body. His response, automatic with years of practice, was immediate. Nose to nose, they grinned. Heat rose between the couple, lovers since college who believed in their wedding vows and never go to bed angry always the plan.

The next morning Steve woke, his heat seeking missile searching for fulfillment from the woman of his dreams. Instead of a naked body curled next to him, he touched a cold pillow and no Sally. The aroma of baking apple dumplings drifted through the open door.

She's up to something, he thought, as his boner wilted like a flower needing water.

He pulled on baggy shorts and a tattered Grateful Dead sweat shirt and barefooted, he followed his nose sniffing all the way to the breakfast nook where he found Sally in a compromising position. She leaned over the table to arrange purple hyacinths and early yellow daffodils picked from a sunny garden close to the house. With her blond hair caught back in a pony tail, she looked like the girl who captured his attention on the campus at New York University many years before. And she still turned him on.

He wrapped his arms around her and assumed a position to make her an offer she couldn't refuse.

As if baked apples were part of the usual Sunday fare, Sally straightened to break the connection and kissed his cheek. "Good morning, sleepy head. Get out of my way or the dumplings will burn. The waffle iron just beeped so breakfast is officially ready."

"What's with all the fancy food this morning? Not that I don't appreciate the flowers and you know how I love your dumplings, sweetheart, but we always have scrambled eggs and bacon."

She unfolded a cloth napkin with a spring motif of birds and butterflies and spread it across her lap. "There is nothing but the best for you, and for us."

After breakfast ended, Steve stretched and rolled his shoulders. "You're right. A small healthy feast on the weekend is special. And listen." He cupped his ear. "What do you hear?"

"Uh, nothing."

"Right. The glorious sound of silence."

Suddenly, a baby nearby began to cry loud. Then a dog barked and didn't stop. From next door, one of the new neighbors, the guy, yelled "Jimmy, stop torturing the dog and Mona, pick up the baby. She needs changing."

Steve exchanged glances with Sally. "About those listings. Are there any for mature adults only?"

"It just so happens. . ."

Chapter 5

An hour later, the Atwood's were on their way to the first corner townhouse on the list. By owner, it said in the paper. Located two towns north of their home and just past Nyack, NY, Sally, always the optimist, had high hopes. They drove into the attractive wooded gated community, followed directions through winding streets, groomed lawns and stopped at the back end of the large property.

"It's so quiet here." Steve got out of the car. Sally joined him. They walked up the flagstone path and he rang the bell. Chimes rang. No one responded. He rang again.

The neighbor next door called out from a window. "Are you the police?"

"No. We came to check out the house. It's for sale."

"Not any more, it isn't at least not for a while. There are rumors about a double murder or something close to it from what I've heard."

Steve shook his head. "So where's the crime scene tape?"

The guy slammed the window down and the Atwood's stood there on a bright spring morning feeling as if they'd been had. By what? They didn't know.

They drove out of the community from hell and didn't stop until they reached a coffee shop a few miles north.

After ordering coffee and lemon meringue pie to share, Steve asked the friendly waitress if she knew anything about a murder, suicide or robbery in the adult community down the road. She bit her full red lips and her bright eyes slid away just for a moment. The Atwood's had read that was a sign she either was about to lie or didn't know.

Pretending to take their order she scribbled on her pad. "I'm not supposed to talk about it or I'll lose my job but there's always something going on over there, especially in the back townhouses. Gossip is like robberies or worse bad stuff."

"Thanks. We won't repeat this." When she hurried to fill their order, Sally frowned. "Let's move on. I think the neighbor was keeping the house for a friend. It's too spooky way back there anyway. Do you agree?"

"Oh, yeah. Move on, Sherlock."

The cottage by the Hudson River appeared to be perfect from the outside with a SOLD sign on the lawn.

Disappointed, Sally checked the list. "Honey, we've looked at two from the outside and already time flies by. There's a town about twenty miles from here. I did some research and this appears to be a great town, taxes low, a 5 star restaurant where people from New York City come to dine, scenic beauty so I think we should give it a look-see."

"What I really want to do is go home and snuggle with you, Sally. That's the truth of it. I hate driving around like this."

"I'll make you a deal, baby. Drive without a fuss or prejudice; keep an open mind and when we're home, we'll snuggle."

"Deal. What's the name of the town so I can program it in the GPS?"

She ran a finger down the copious list. "River's Edge."

The gas guzzling Mercedes tank was filled and the GPS lady took command. The Atwood's named her Mother for

Steve's bossy mom who knew everything, just ask her. Passed on a year ago, beloved by her only son, Sally, the daughter-in-law and three grandchildren, Granny Atwood had had a great sense of humor and got a kick out of the GPS lady.

Mother barked out orders. "Turn North to merge onto the Palisade Parkway. Drive twenty miles until you see the sign River's Edge. Drive 0.1 mile and you are at your destination."

They laughed. "Thanks, Mother. You're always right."

Sally said, "What if she replied? "Yes, I am.""

"I wouldn't be surprised. How she put up with Dad always amazed me."

The scenery changed driving north. There were more pine trees. Everything seemed more lush, less citified with banks of spring flowers blooming along the highway. As they neared the town, they heard waterfalls rushing down a stream, crashing against rocks and boulders.

Mother announced they had reached their destination. "Let's park and walk to get a feel of the town. Thank you, Mother."

They found a town parking lot, slid two dollars worth of coins in, locked up and began to survey the situation.

"Look, there's a cottage called The Pet Emporium. Isn't that cute?"

"Very cute but we don't have a dog or cat."

"Well, there's that. We could check out the shop. It looks charming."

"Sure. Keep walking. And here's a realtor's office. Should we go in now?"

Steve stopped. He looked in the window. A woman smiled and waved for them to come in. And that's what they did.

Trumbull Realtor's had wood paneled walls and carpeted floors with a lemon scent in the air. The busy office had several clients leaning over desks, pointing at pictures and asking questions of the staff. The attractive gray haired woman who waved to them turned out to be the manager, Claudia Wilcox.

"Hi. Sit you down and rest a spell while I see how I can make your life better."

Steve exchanged glances with Sally. "We just came over to see what River's Edge is all about."

"We're all about value and the good life."

Tired, eager to move on, Steve answered her questions while Sally took notes. She had a good feeling about the town and they'd been there less than fifteen minutes.

"First, I must tell you we're just looking since we own a home in Rockland County and all of a sudden my wife," he touched Sally's hand, "tells me the house is too big now that the kids have grown up and moved out."

Sally added," And before they decide to move back in."

Claudia laughed so hard, her glasses slipped off and fell to the floor just the way her boss Jim used to. Picking them up, she placed them further back on her pert nose. "I've seen that happen all too often. Once the children move out, they should be on their own." She circled around her desk to sit with them eliminating a barrier. "Ice tea, coffee, lemonade? We have a selection of homemade goodies."

"Yes to lemonade and goodies whatever they are. I smell chocolate chip cookies nearby."

"Steve, we're watching our weight."
"Honey, watch your own weight today. I need a snack to ease the stress I'm under. Claudia understands. Right?"

The manager was off to the hospitality set-up and back with Steve's request plus an extra glass of lemonade for Sally, the reluctant wife.

They sipped and munched, chatting like old friends and slowly the Atwood's told the kind shrewd woman what they might be interested in subject to selling their home, of course.

"Two bedrooms, two baths, a kitchen big enough for two."

Sally interjected. "I'd like a room with a sun roof and also a small deck and a yard in case we ever get a dog."

"What's with a sun roof? The sun's outside. You want sun, go out where the sun is."

Claudia, comfortable with the Atwood's, put her two cents in. "Children, play nice, don't fight."

Her comment brought a burst of laughter from the three of them. Sally dried her eyes from laughing. "Oh my. We don't usually bicker."

"In public. Make love not war is our motto."

"Yes, well getting back to property, do you have an idea about price range?"

Steve wrote down his yearly salary, savings, equity and whatever else the realtor needed. She thought for a minute, went to a filing cabinet and returned with folders to sit behind her desk. Her computer had the multiple listing open and they leaned forward to listen and learn. One important fact was that Trumbull Realtor also had agreements to sell houses for their clients who wanted to move to Rivers Edge but hadn't sold their home yet.

Steve reached for another cookie and grinned. "We've come to the right place, Sally."

His wife of many years nodded and hoped for the best.

"Are you ready for a tour of some reasonably priced smaller homes nearby?"

"That's what we came for."

They piled into Claudia's comfortable BMW SUV. She pointed out places of interest including the well know restaurant The River's Edge and chattered on about the falls. Before long she made a right turn into a wooded community with separate homes, well -tended lawns and an activity center.

"This is a mature adults only community, fifty five years and up, no grandchildren living here only to visit. Strict rules about that. That building," she gestured to the white circular structure, "houses the activity center where they have comprehensive daily programs and often authors are invited to speak, cooking classes and so much more. And there's a pool and eight HarTru tennis courts so easy on older bones."

She pulled up to a home and Sally's heart beat faster. Excited, she got out of the big SUV first. Her eyes widened and took in the spring flowers, a flagstone path without weeds growing between the flat stones, tulips pushing the way through a garden alongside daffodils and huge bushes with buds promising a harvest of flowers. She calmed herself. *Check out the inside, how much, can they afford it and what time can they move in,* she thought. *Or maybe someone was murdered there and no one wanted to buy it so this was a bargain they couldn't refuse. NOT!*

Claudia opened the door. No lock box here. "I always think it's silly when a realtor points to the bathroom and says this is the bathroom. So I suggest you take your time to wander around and call for me when you have questions."

"Great." Steve grabbed Sally by the hand and step by step they examined every room. The carpets were in pristine condition as were the bathrooms', one adjoining the master bedroom had a Jacuzzi tub and double sink. The basement was spotless. The kitchen had an entrance to the attached garage to fit two cars with tools hung neatly. They walked out to the deck overlooking the yard. To their surprise it was fenced in with white pickets. Sally envisioned a dog or two. She forgot about a sun roof. A room upstairs could suffice as an office or whatever. Now they'd talk business with Claudia or look at more homes.

"Be cool. Don't look too excited." Steve squeezed her hand.

Their new found friend and realtor held their future in the palm of her hand when they entered the living room where she sat as if she owned the place.

"The house is nice, very clean and just how old is it and what's the asking price?"

Steve towered over the petite woman who seemed to be comfortable in her own skin.

"Sit you down and let's talk. This home is ten years old. Nothing has to be renovated since it's what we call almost new. But it isn't new and so the asking price is reduced. If the price is more than you can afford, come up with an offer and we'll see if the owner agrees. As far as your present home, I'm certain I can arrange to flip or sell before too long. You say it's in an established community with young people moving in?"

"Yes. That's what prompted us to search for another smaller house with no school taxes."

"Good. I've got the picture." She shuffled through some paper. "The owner is asking this." She showed them the figure. "Take a walk, talk it over and come back to me before we move on. I'll be right here making calls."

Stunned, Steve staggered out to the deck and slumped into a lawn chair. "What did we pay for our house, Sally?"

"Honey, thirty years ago a hundred thousand dollars was a big deal and we got a beautiful house to raise three kids in. I stayed home and slaved. Now prices have sky rocketed. Claudia told us the asking price. That means it's negotiable if we want it." Leaning close, Sally kissed him full on the lips.

Already his five o'clock shadow had begun to sprout. Birds flocked to the tall post feeder, Robin Red Breasts flitted back and forth, flapping their wings. Steve squinted to see a family of rabbits scurry across the far end of the fence, small gray fur against white pickets.

"It's like a Disney movie back here. I expect Snow White to dance out any minute."

"Me, too. So what do you think? Look at more houses or go with our feelings?"

Steve hugged Sally around her waist. "I've never gone wrong with my feelings, baby. Let's go in and see what happens next."

Claudia Wilcox had been in the business a long time. She could tell by the pace of their footsteps, they loved the house. An offer was going to be on the table in two minutes or less. Wisely she'd bought another house after the purchase of this one and it was time to move on. The Atwood's were likeable. They'd bring vitality necessary to Rivers Edge, always a concern as Jim Trumbull taught her when she was but a newbie. At this moment she felt like Bloody Mary in South Pacific offering her beautiful daughter to the Lieutenant. "You Like? You Buy?" Shaking the music and words from her head, the realtor stood to greet them.

"Have you come to a conclusion or shall we look at some other properties?

Steve puffed out his chest, alpha male taking a stance. "We're gonna make you an offer you can't refuse."

When the laughter subsided and numbers were scribbled on a page back and forth, Claudia nodded. "The owner agrees to this figure."

"So soon? How do you know?" Sally radiated with happiness.

"I'm the owner."

Shaking hands all around knowing there was much more to discuss and papers to sign and what happens to their other house, Claudia herded the excited couple into her over-large vehicle and left the community to drive back to the office. Twilight descended early. The town took on a fairy tale quality as light sparkled from old fashioned lamp posts down Main Street.

"Let's keep this simple, folks. We'll sign some preliminary papers and before you leave, I'll call my good friend Larry Owens at The River's Edge Restaurant for a table for two overlooking the falls. The treats on me. When you get home, FAX papers on your home right away so I can get busy. If you don't have a lawyer for all of this legal nonsense, I can get you one of the best and most reasonable one in town. In fact, I hold a marker on him. It just might be payback time."

Sally begged off when Steve went to the men's room. "Sorry we can't take you up on your generous dinner invitation. We want to get home before rush hour. Sometime this next week we'll return to solidify plans. And thanks so much for your generosity."

Hugging her new clients, the manager of Trumbull Realtor sighed and leaned back in Jim Trumbull's worn leather chair. After they drove off she couldn't stop smiling. "Thanks, Coach," she whispered, "you taught me kindness goes a long way."

Chapter 6

No dusting and minimal cleaning today, Sally thought, as she jogged through the streets of the old neighborhood past shiny new swing sets, unlined faces of young women pushing twin strollers with either twins or little ones born close together. Head held high, she waved a mental farewell to thirty years spent here and planned a luncheon with her closest friends. All but a few had moved to Florida and Arizona to live out their lives with their children visiting once or twice a year.

This is not what she and Steve had in mind. Their idea was to visit their kids once in a while and go to plays on Broadway. She envisioned starting over in Rivers Edge, getting a job, giving back to a welcoming community.

A half hour later Sally arrived home after the best workout in months to find Steve's car in the driveway. She stopped, frightened. Fear flooded through her. Emergency ran through her mind. She raced in the house calling, "Steve, Steve." No answer.

Up the stairs to the bedroom she ran and found him lying there on the bed face ashen, tie askew.

"What happened? Are you sick? Should I call 911?"

He struggled to sit up. "I'm sick all right. I got to work. A note from Hiro San lay on my desk. He's the top boss now. I didn't have a clue as to why he wanted to see me early in the day but I hurried over to his closed door. What came next gave me the shock of my entire working career. "Steven San," he said with a smile, "We must close your division of the company. Therefore you are now retired." He wiped sweat from his brow. "I collapsed in a chair and listened. We give you superior retirement package and you keep new car fully paid. One hitch as you say here in America, Steven San.

Arrangement is top secret. Company has been informed you requested retirement as of today. Not to reveal you leaving otherwise to anyone." Then Hori San, the snake, I never liked him, pushed a paper across the desk and said, "Sign here, keep pen."

"What did you do?"

"I had no choice. I signed, accepted a folder with pages of information and with much bowing on his part, I left—out of work for the first time in my life."

Shocked by the sudden turn of events, Sally turned when she heard her husband's wracking sobs. She held him, patting his back the way she'd done a million times for their children over a broken toy or a boo boo.

"Steve, we'll find a way to survive. Let's look at the damn folder and figure out how we'll manage before you get a job and I can work. This is no time to move." Her dreams of River Edge faded.

"NO. It's an omen. Sometimes an ill wind blows good. Someone said that, I think." He sat up straight, resolution in his face. "Actually I'm tired of traveling every week. Since 9/11, air travel is complicated. Safety first but It used to be so easy. Did you FAX the information to Claudia?"

"Of course. I'm very efficient. What else can I do right now."

Steve's eyes got that gleam in his eyes. "How about this?" He tugged her running bra down and helped her pull down the damp tights after she kicked off her sneakers. "Lose the socks, Sally, while I peel off this damn suit. I hope my next job doesn't require a tie."

"Nude modeling, maybe?"

"Nah."

"Shower first?"

"No time, sweetheart. Too much love happening to stop right now."

In the afterglow, Steve revealed a secret he'd kept hidden from his wife and himself for a long time. "I have a confession to make, honey. Please listen and don't hate me."

An affair, a hidden family, he's gay? Sally hid her panic, drew the sheet up to her chin and like the good wife she'd learned to be, she paid close attention.

"I've been in the Security division of several companies for years. That's my specialty and always as the capo de tutti capo manager; the go-to guy for problems. Meanwhile I let computer skills slip since I always had someone else handling that skill for me. Here comes the big letdown. Changes in equipment have advanced so fast that I'm left behind without the skills needed to apply for another position somewhere. An old dog without new tricks, that's me. No one will hire me despite my great resume; not when they find out I'm lacking. . ."

"Honey, if this is what's troubling you all I can say is stop beating yourself up. It's no biggie. I have skills. My computer dances for me. We'll find a way."

"Oh. No biggie, huh." He ran his fingers through shaggy gray hair. "Okay. How about buying a fixer upper?" Without waiting for an answer, a naked Steve trotted over to the office and called their favorite realtor.

My husband's crazy, Sally thought as the shower set to high pounded semi-hot water down. Worried, she dried her hair and dressed in faded jeans and a long sleeve pink tee shirt with a big heart on the front. You Gotta Have Heart with musical notes sprinkled around decorated the old shirt.

"Coffee's on. I had Wheaties and strawberries. We have an appointment with Claudia at one o' clock. She said there were a few fixer uppers for sale." He turned to look into space. "I thought I heard her snicker as I hung up."

"Good, honey, I'll be ready." *Snicker,* Sally thought, *I bet she laughed her head off.*

Vitamins and a bowl of Rice Chex with sliced strawberries were just enough for her this morning. By the time Steve barreled downstairs, Sally was outside waiting in the paid up BMW, the retirement folder in one hand and photos and complete information about the home they currently lived in the other hand.

By the time they reached River's Edge, Sally understood exactly where they were with the financial package. No more wifey for her. She had to be a partner with Steve in every way in their new life. In the parking lot, Sally stopped her husband before he opened the driver's door.

"You're depressed and it's more than losing your job, isn't it?" He avoided her intense gaze and nodded. "What else troubles you, love?"

His chest rose and fell before he opened up. "It's the kids. I don't know why we went through all the trouble and expense to have them only to watch as they waved goodbye. Lisa, my baby girl, allowed that no good Donald to drag her off to Silicon Valley in God Damn California where we're not going, followed by Melissa living in Costa Rica working for an advertising company with Georgio. They'll have babies we'll never see. So I ask you, what's it all about? Having children only to watch them fly away to be seen whenever. And now our son, John, pardon me, Jonathon changes his name. Sally, I'm heartsick . We've wasted our youth and money over these kids and they're strangers to us."

"So that's it."

"Yeah."

"You're not alone, Steve. I bet parents everywhere experience the same sense of loss when their children move on. It sucks. And yet we love our privacy now, right?"

"Hmm. I guess so."

"Sex whenever we're in the mood with no interruptions?"

He grinned. "That works."

"So try to get over it. I think you've got long delayed post partum blues."

"I'll try."

Chapter 7

The wide Main Street bustled with energy on this Monday morning. People waved driving by to friends; dogs kept up a lively pace to the left of their owner's side.

"Bucolic is the word that comes to me."

"And orderly. The air smells sweet up here." Sally inhaled the soft spring air and exhaled. "Just wonderful"

The Atwood's entered Trumbull Realtor to the musical tinkle of a bell.

A smiling Claudia's face changed to concern. "Sit you down. I see you're in good humor yet I sense a change. Something's happened."

Sally whispered, "How did you know?"

Claudia shook her head. "Don't ask. It's like a sixth sense. Tell or don't tell. It's personal. Whatever I can do to ease your pain is yours for the asking." She smiled and got down to business. "Steve, you mentioned a fixer upper. We have several available." She tapped a folder on the desk. "I caution you about buying such a home. It's fine for a young couple starting up with carpentry skills and pals to help paint, saw, tear down and whatever has to be accomplished to make a home liveable. My question is do you have carpentry skills?" She focused on Steve.

Crestfallen, he shook his head. "Other than hanging a picture and hammering my thumb, I have to admit the answer is no."

"Many men think they can do just about everything and they can't. Earning a living is primary. So let me warn you, to fix such a house could run into big bucks. Even a small dump with honest carpenters and painters might run into maybe two hundred thou. I've seen it happen. So if you want to take a look, let's go." She rose, grabbed her handbag and strode to the door.

Sally took Steve by the hand. "Honey, from what Claudia just said, someday we might need the money to have us a re-haul like a fixer upper."

"You mean our bodies?"

"Oh yeah. Hip replacement, knees get cooked, rotator cuffs tear. Steve," Sally clutched his arm, "Soon our bodies will need replacement parts like cars going in and out of the shop. I've heard when you reach sixty five, watch out."

"I thought the words golden oldies applied to us. And suddenly we're here. What the hell happened?"

"Age happened. It creeps up while you're busy living. Claudia, we've changed our minds. We will buy your home."

Steve stumbled over to the hospitality table to catch his breath. *Calm down,* he thought and poured lemonade in two glasses and happily placed a handful of chocolate chip cookies, still warm from someone's oven, on a plate. He munched cookies and listened to his wife suddenly take over. He, the alpha male who had always taken care of his family financially and in every other way, sat like a kid eating cookies while his wife discussed business. The big business of purchasing a house.

"Pardon me, folks. You're talking about a husband who has lost his job so no longer do we have the stability we had before. I don't see our way clear to purchase a home let alone go out for dinner. Sally, before long, we might have to declare bankruptcy. We've been so careless with credit cards, at this point I don't know how much we owe. Sorry Claudia. This is too personal to discuss in front to you."

Sally's face lost the rosy glow she'd felt on the drive up. Her husband had gone off his rocker, thrown for a loop since losing his job this morning. The shock scared her, too.

Still calm, as if she'd heard this story many times, the kind realtor touched Steve's hand. "We have a financial advisor on staff. May I call him in for a personal consultation at no expense to you? He came to us from Harvard Business. Sean Adler has worked wonders for our clients."

"Excuse us for a family discussion." Sally grabbed Steve's hand to move to a corner while Claudia snipped the ends off long stemmed purple Irises and set them in a deep glass vase half filled with water.

"What have we stumbled into in this small town?" She didn't wait for an answer. "Honey, we should accept the kindness of strangers and see what happens. You have a pension, your health, and me. A job is around the corner for a man with your experience. Let's give it a try." Steve shrugged and followed Sally's lead.

"Bring on your Sean Adler. We're ready to make an attempt to solve our problems."

"Sally's the optimist in the family. Her half glass full just overflowed and I'm going with her this time."

"Thanks for your vote of confidence." Claudia gave them a thumbs up and pushed a button. A moment later the most unlikely young man slouched in wearing low slung jeans, a crisp white shirt, sleeves rolled up and a lopsided grin.

"Hey, Miz and Mr. Atwood, pleased to meet you. C'mon back to my cave. I'm working my way up the Trumbull ladder."

The Atwood's exchanged glances.

"He's no older than Johnny."

"Maybe younger."

Over his broad shoulder, Sean said, "Twenty-eight and super smart, tops in my class. So why am I here in River's Edge instead of in the big city, you might ask. The answer's that I liked what I heard about this town and thought I'd give it a shot instead of being a small fish in a big pond." Then he laughed. "Big fat lie. The boss is my mom. She taught me everything I know and then some except what I learned at Harvard Business."

Sean's cave had a butter yellow leather couch, two matching chairs and a desk. His many achievements were framed in dark brown wood. Family pictures of two small children, a honey blond wife and a smiling younger Claudia adorned the polished desk.

His computer hummed, ready to go.

"Tell me your story, bring it up to date as of right now. Ready, set, go."

Sean's fingers flew across the keyboard as Steve opened up in a way Sally had never seen him do before except to her, in private. Sean had garnered their trust in a short time.

After an hour, Sean grinned and rubbed his hands together. "We're in business, folks. Steve, you have no financial worries and your aging benefits are secure. Do you want to work or play golf and hang out?"

"Are you kidding? I love to work, make a living and feel useful. I don't know what hanging out means."

"Oh yeah. Just like Mom." He turned to Sally. "And you, lovely lady? Do you have a plan?"

"Smooth talker, Sean, I can write news articles and have several skills but I'm not sure what I'd like to focus on. Once the old house is sold and we move in to the new one, I'll look around. I call myself a work in progress."

"So there's hope." Steve rose from the comfortable chair and stretched.

"More than hope. I'm making a promise that in a couple of months," he flipped a calendar with gorgeous pictures of dogs and cats on it, the Pet Emporium stamped across the top, "by midsummer the latest, you'll feel right at home in River's Edge."

"You're also an optimist, Sean, like my wife."

"No. I'm a realist." They shook hands.

"About your family pictures, at your age, you already have children."

"Michael's two, Kimberly is one." His voice softened as he said their names. "Keep us busy. They're a joy. Well, thanks for entering my cave to allow me into your personal world. All information is private and will not be available to anyone except for head honcho. If necessary, I'll be in touch. I do hope I'll see you again real soon."

After a brief meeting with their new favorite friendly realtor, The Atwood's decided to have an early dinner at the River's Edge Restaurant where they were greeted by the owner, Larry Owens. The rugged man stood tall on the path, a yellow Labrador Retriever by his left side.

"Welcome to River's Edge where the elite meet to eat. This is Sam. He doesn't bite, much."

"Claudia Wilcox suggested we come over before we head back to Rockland County. I'm Steve Atwood. This is my wife Sally." They shook hands on a glorious sunny late afternoon.

"So you'll be moving up here?"

"Possibly. Right now we're hungry and we've heard about the view so we'd like to eat outside if there's a table available."

"At this time of day, I'm sure there is. Follow me. Heel, Sam." The big dog rose obediently and moved close to Larry Owens side.

They sank into comfortable chairs, thrilled by the sweet air; the rush of melted snow cascaded down the stream in a roar as it smashed against the rocks and boulders.

"What do you think so far, Steve? Is this wonderful or what?"

"Pinch me. I'm dreaming. How about filet mignon with stuffed baked potatoes?"

"Stuffed with what?"

"I don't know. You take over. I want to sit back and listen to the falls." He closed his eyes to ponder over the events that lead up to this moment in just two days. *First Sally said the neighborhood had changed with young people moving in with babies. Then she said the deck had rotted, the roof needed new shingles and let's look at houses. Now I'm forced to retire, out of a job and obsolete. All in one weekend. What's the old joke? Oh yeah, "Aside from that Mrs. Lincoln, how did you like the play?"*

Steve's nose twitched. Food alert. His eyes opened to see oysters on a small plate set before him.

Sally grinned as she dipped a big shrimp in sauce and chewed the tail end. "Delicious. Did you doze for a few minutes while I ordered?"

"No." He used the tines of the small fork to lift the oyster and dip it in a succulent butter sauce. A quick thrust into his mouth and Sally heard a moan of delight. He blotted a drip of sauce from his chin. "Delectable. To continue, I mentally recounted the past few days. It's been a whirlwind and I think it will definitely blow harder until we settle down."

His wife of many years nodded agreement. "What's your take on young Sean?"

"I'm impressed. He's knowledgeable, you saw his credits, pleasant and damn smart."

"Even though Claudia is his mother, I still don't get why he's in River's Edge. It's a small town for someone of his talents."

"It's not our problem, Sally. Concentrate on us."

The table was cleared by unnoticed hands while they talked and the main course, small filet mignon wrapped in bacon done to perfection was placed before them. Twice baked potatoes with steamed broccoli were offered as side dishes.

"What did I do to deserve this?"

"You married me."

Steve moved his seat closer and gave his wife a passionate kiss. "I have the urge to make love to you right now, sweetheart."

"Must be the oysters. On the other hand, filet mignon always turns me on." Sally sliced into the medium rare meat. Juices flowed. She chewed and savored. "It's like butter, honey."

Unaware that Larry Owens kept his eyes on them, the Atwood's finished the best dinner ever and left with many thanks, leaving a generous tip for the waiter.

HOUSEBROKEN

The owner of one of the finest restaurant's north of New York City jotted down a few observations about the pleasant mature couple who may soon be a part of the community thanks to Claudia Wilcox. *If only she'd look at him as more than a friend. Damn. Try, try again, Larry.* River's Edge needed quality energetic people. He recalled his good friend Jim Trumbull bringing a young woman in for dinner long ago. What a boost to the town when Jim and Grace Meredith partnered in The Pet Emporium, got married and made a good life here until Jim passed on. Larry poured single malt and toasted to his friend, thoughts of Claudia still on his mind.

"I'm ready."

"Again? You know it takes a while for me to regroup, honey."

Sally punched her horny husband in the arm and giggled. After the ride home, a dash to the bedroom with clothes abandoned on the stairs, they'd fallen into each others' arms. "I meant I'm ready to move so let's call Claudia tomorrow and ask how soon we can start the process. They said they'd find a buyer without a problem."

"You might be naïve. I think it takes longer to make arrangements, sell our old house and move." From her sigh, Steve knew his wife needed encouragement. "Okay. I'll call tomorrow and get a time frame. Now snuggle up and let's get to sleep. We had a great day."

"Yes, we certainly did."

Chapter 8

Behind Claudia's closed door, Sean slouched in brown leather chair and crossed his long legs at the ankles.

"What's your gut feeling about the Atwoods?" Claudia sat opposite the handsome young man with the tousled blond hair, computer at the ready.

"They have potential, Moms."

She sat up straight and wagged a finger at him. "Sean, I've told you a million times the word potential is not clear enough. Illuminate me as in "accentuate the positive, eliminate the negative, latch on to the affirmative and don't mess with Mr. in between." She paused, listening to something Sean couldn't hear. "That's from a song my parents used to jive to way long ago. I must get a copy of that tune. It's from 1944."

"Oh, Moms, unless your office is bugged, I don't like anyone to know when you holler at me. I'm not a kid anymore. So," he grinned the lop-sided smile she could never resist since he was an infant, "How am I doing?"

"Way cool, honey. Let's boogie before my back gives out."

Sean pushed the button for the oldies station. The BeeGees sang How Deep is Your Love from Saturday Night Fever. "Disco, Moms?"

Mother and son danced around the spacious room until Sean noticed beads of perspiration on his mother's brow.

"Let's sit for few. I've got to get home soon, so talk business." They settled in to the comfortable repartee cultivated over the years. "I'm thinking about a flip with the Atwood's house. A quick turnover . A new roof courtesy of our favorite contactor and the deck done in a day by um…"

"George Mellin. He's fast, competent and available. I like to throw a job his way whenever we can."

"And I know just the couple. Remember the Shores ? Mel and Linda. She's expecting and Mel Jr. is three. He needs to work closer to his job in Rockland County. All I need is a painter." He stared off in some middle distance then snapped his fingers. "Steve Atwood."

"Steve Atwood what?"

"He'll do it. Even if he never lifted a brush, I'll make him an offer he can't refuse." Whistling the theme from The Godfather, he waved goodbye.

Claudia sat on the leather couch and watched the impression shaped by her son's body fill in. Memories swept over her. She thought about her husband, Kenny and felt old tears well up. They were short of milk and coffee. Kenny said he'd be right back and drove through the sudden snowstorm. She said, "Be careful, honey." An hour later or maybe two when a policeman knocked on the door, the snow had escalated to blizzard proportions.

"Sorry for your loss," he said. She didn't know what he meant. He handed her a note found in Kenny's pocket. Sloan's Market Coffee—Breakfast blend, cream, Oatmeal. "Yes, this is the grocery list I wrote but …"

"One car accident. Skidded on the ice over the railing and down into the stream."

At least she thinks that's what the cop said. Widowed, alone, now what? Life ended for Claudia Wilcox, too, until Jim Trumbull dragged her back, gave her a job and taught her the Realtor business. A few months later, a phone call came from Sister Mary Teresa at St. Paul's, the kind nun who had helped the young widow through many grim nights and days.

"A baby boy has been left here, sure to be swept into the system to an unknown future unless you open your broken heart, young lady."

Heart racing, Claudia drove to the church. Snow fell. She slipped on the path to St. Paul's. Inside the hallowed hall, the young widow wiped her boots and waited. Sister Teresa hurried toward her, a blue bundle in her arms. Claudia read the name tag. Sean Adler 8lb 6oz 2/13/1992. How would she manage? After a year of filling out forms, home and character inspections, the adoption was complete. Mother and child reunion as Simon and Garfunkel foreshadowed in their wonderful song.

Yet twenty eight years later, here they sat, mother and son, grandmother to his sweet little kids. At fifty- two, she had no time for anything but business and raising Sean. Loneliness crept over her after Sean closed the door. Her son has a wife and two small children. In truth, did she really want to spend the rest of her life without a mate?

Crossing the spacious room to the bathroom, she opened the door. The automatic light came on. It was time to assess her face. She peered close to get a good look. At fifty-two, she viewed laugh lines and crow's feet. Whoever designated the word crow's feet to eye crinkles should be electrocuted. *Not bad for an old broad*, she thought. *Actually kind of cute. Nose still turned up just a bit; apple cheeks rosy thanks to blush stuff*. Claudia backed up to survey her shape. She sucked in her gut and turned to profile her figure.

"Well, all right. I'm good to go as they say and who the hell are *they*?" Claudia said. "Maybe I'll ask Larry Owens for a date. I've refused him for too many years."

She speed dialed his number. "Larry Owens, please. Claudia Wilcox here."

"Claudia, it's so, uh, nice to hear from you. Do you want me to comp a prospective customer? We're slow tonight."

"Larry, I accept your invitation for a date."

"Date? Which one? There were so many."

"Let's start from the first invitation when Sean was about two. He's twenty-eight now. You're still single?"

"I am."

"So am I. Are you free to go out tonight?"

"It just so happens I can arrange for Conrad to cover for me."

"Good. Pick me up in an hour. Oh, do you know where I live?"

"I certainly do."

"And do you like movies?"

"Movies?"

She giggled like a young girl. "Movies where you buy two tickets and eat popcorn. Like that."

His masculine laugh made her tingle all over.

"Sounds like fun. I'll see you in an hour." Larry Owens stared at the phone. He waved to the maitre de, Conrad who responded right away. "I have a pressing engagement and must leave right away. You're in charge. I trust you to take care of River's Edge Finest Restaurant. Close up on time; call my accountant to do the tabs. Make sure the kitchen staff cleans up as always. You will collect a bonus for this extra responsibility so do it well. Thank you. See you tomorrow."

Larry Owens, his faithful companion Sam panting by his side, drove to the lonely place he called home. Grinning, he thought, *I have a pressing engagement.* And hoped so.

Chimes rang out. Larry straightened his shoulders, took a deep breath and exhaled. The scent of mint from the breath gizmo melted in his mouth. The moment he'd waited for at hand and now what? He'd forgotten how to talk, smile, tell stories, jokes, laugh.

The door opened and the woman he'd dreamed of for years stood before him.

Larry dropped the bunch of spring flowers on the floor and held her in his arms. "Claudia, it's been a long, long..."

"Time." She cried into his shirt and lifted her face. "See what you've made me do? I put on make-up and eye cream and now I'm a mess."

One kiss led to another. Starved for affection, they moved toward more advanced touch and feel until she broke away. "Movies?" They laughed knowing maybe next time. "Are you hungry?"

"Claudia, I've hungered for you a long time so right now if you'd like to try a special wine I brought from River's Edge Finest and some cheese and crackers to match, we can get acquainted again."

"Yes, that's a perfect way to start our evening. Now pick up the flowers and follow me."

Chapter 9

Once Claudia gave the Atwoods the all clear to start packing, they stood in the middle of their living room not knowing where to begin.

"Hoarders." Sally sagged against her husband ready to cry. "Thirty years of hoarding qualifies us as hoarders from hell. How do we begin to tackle all of this junk?"

"Not to worry, my love. Working for the Japanese all my life, they made sure everything extraneous had to be swept clean before the next product came on the shelf and I was the coordinator in charge." He rolled up his sleeves and made a list. "We'll tackle one room at a time."

They attacked the tedious process in a logical organized way. Steve brought free boxes home from the local booze shop and Sally retrieved old boxes from the garage. They worked as a team just like old times when they first moved in. Over a quick lunch, Steve looked up from the possible dusty old giveaway book he was about to toss in a box.

"Now that I'm unemployed, I'm thinking about writing."

Sally almost choked on the grilled cheese sandwich she'd just bitten into to. "Write? Write about what?"

"A memoir."

"A memoir about. . ."

"My years of work. You know. As part of a corporation."

She couldn't stop herself from the laugh that bubbled up and exploded at the foolish idea.

"Why are you laughing?"

"Steve, you were the manager of sales and checked invoices. You made a fine salary and took care of your family but that's hardly worth a memoir."

"Oh. I guess I'll have to find another occupation." He finished his sandwich. "Maybe I'll service the good women up in River's Edge. You can write a recommendation of fine results for over thirty years."

She scrambled across a stack of books and clothes to attack him. "I'm sorry I laughed. You know I love and respect you, sweetheart." Sally kissed him all over his sweaty face. "Just remember our wedding vows or I'll kill you, my love." They continued to discard and pack.

Daylight faded into twilight. Steve's stomach grumbled. "Did you hear that? Food. I need food, woman."

"I'm on a roll so don't bother me. There's cold chicken in the fridge and salad fixings. Besides, I want to lose ten pounds before we move."

"Sally, stop worrying about your weight. You can spend your time getting skinny when you're dead."

She hurled the book in her hand at his head and missed. An old cushion about to go in the discard pile came next. This one hit Steve's head and feathers flew. He threw it back and soon they were laughing, covered in white fluffy feathers.

"We sound like an old radio show my folks listened to."

Steve spit out a feather and nodded. "The Bickersons. I think the actor's were, uh..."

"Don Ameche and Frances Langford. And then there was another show with Alice Faye and Phil Harris. Mom liked them better. They were funny."

"Sally," he pulled her close, feathers and all, "I don't want us to be like the Bickersons or other couples who are spiteful and caustic with each other. Like Claudia Wilcox said, play nice, don't fight. We love each other. Right?"

"You betcha. Now get in the kitchen and slice enough chicken for me. Whistle when dinner's ready. I'm hungry." Striking a seductive pose, Sally quoted a line from *To Have and Have Not*, one of their favorite old movies. "You know how to whistle, don't you? Just pucker up and blow." When she emphasized the word blow, feathers rose and fell. Again the Atwoods laughed. Steve climbed down the attic ladder still chuckling.

Sally peered around at all the feathers. "I'll sweep and you do the food. How's that for a switcheroo?" No answer from the kitchen. She smiled. They worked so well together. Most of the time.

A chef's hat perched at a jaunty angle on Steve's head. With a graceful gesture, he waved his wife to slide into her side of the breakfast nook. An attempt to spin around for the salad almost landed him on the tile floor. Quick thinking and his out stretched hand grabbed the counter and Steve was on two feet to return with a bowl topped with a circle of black olives.

Sally's eyes widened. "How pretty. I didn't expect such a fancy salad."

"Taste it. See if it's as good as it looks."

After the first few forks full and much moaning in appreciation, she nodded. "I taste avocado slices, tomato, red onion thinly cut, Romaine topped with shredded mozzarella, just enough chicken also cut thin and then the big black pitted olives I love. Steve, you're a marvel."

"Yes, I am. And I told you I could cook." They ate in the companionable silence married couples often enjoy.

After lunch Sally stifled the urge to say, "Making a salad is not cooking." She'd save that for another time.

Two weeks later, the moving truck pulled up. The Atwoods were packed and ready to leave the old homestead. A young couple had come by with Sean Adler from Trumbull Realtor and just as promised, they'd made a deal. On the drive to River's Edge, Sally scribbled a note. **Priority: Call the kids**.

As if he read her mind, Steve said, "Call the kids. We don't want them showing up at our doorstep in Rockland County to find we don't live there."

"Never happen, honey. They're too preoccupied with themselves to think about us." A sore point for her dear husband. Her cell phone played a demanding tune. Sally hit the button. "Hello?"

"Mom, it's Jonathon."

"Who?"

"Your son. Uh, John. Johnny."

"Yes, honey. You sound upset." She mouthed to Steve, "It's our son."

"I'm coming home, Mom." She whispered, "He wants to come home." A swerve of the car and Steve sped up.

"Why? What's wrong? You just got married, moved out and joined a law firm."

"Tiffany hates me." Their only son sobbed.

"Johnny, we're on the way to a town upstate. River's Edge is the name. We sold the house and bought a nice small house up here."

"You sold the house? Without asking me? Now I have no home and no wife."

"Johnny, stop it right now and get a grip. You have a job, an apartment and you and Tiffany can work things out just the way your father and I did years ago. Meanwhile, if you want to help us move in, here's our new address." She gave it to him. "Call later. Meanwhile we have a full day's work ahead of us. Take care and always remember we love you."

"Damn it. Just when we thought the coast was clear. . ."

"Honey, we have our hands full with our own lives right now."

Spring had come into full bloom driving north. A riot of wild flowers cascaded along the drive on the Palisade Parkway. Yellow, purple, pink colors blending into one gorgeous blur as they sped along, leading the moving truck toward River's Edge. A rain shower ahead and suddenly rainbows appeared. Not one but two and three. So perfect. A shiver of pleasure ran through Sally. She touched her husband's arm and knew he experienced the same.

When they pulled up to the new house, Claudia, Sean and his family were there to greet them, and the delicious aroma of apple pie baking in the oven hung in the air.

"We planned to have the band roll out but they were busy, so it's just us." Sean strummed on his guitar and they sang a funny song he made up about welcome to our town, it's a very, very good town. The blond baby girl sang the loudest to finish with a burp.

"Kimberly says she's sorry for the burp." The two year old boy patted his sister.

"Hi, I'm Marlena, mom, wife and lawyer. Let's help you get settled."

"Thanks for the wonderful welcome. All boxes are labeled. We'll need some furniture since we gave our old pieces to needy groups. There must be a furniture store nearby."

"Not to worry, Sally." Claudia removed packages from Sally's arms. "Our goal is to get you settled today. Sean has a few friends due here any minute. Muscle guys from the gym."

"Pinch me. I must be dreaming. No one has ever shown so much hospitality before." She pulled Steve close to her side. "This is like the old days when people reached out and helped each other."

Her strong husband nodded. "Yeah. Just like the old days."

"The kindness of strangers is what we do here in River's Edge. Let's get to work. Sally, come with me. The pies are ready. Take the kids so they won't get in the way."

Kimberly snuggled into Sally's neck and Michael reached for her hand. Sally remembered the long ago feeling of small needy babies. How she'd loved and cared for them. *You never forget*, and followed their efficient grandmother into the their new home.

A corner with some toys for Michael to play with and a play crib for the baby to nap were set up and out of the way of traffic. The baby girl went down without a struggle and her sturdy big brother sat cross legged on the floor nearby surrounded with trucks, cars and a miniature train set.

"Of course, they're not always so compliant. You know that having three of your own." Claudia turned off the oven, pulled on mitts and carefully pulled out four apple pies.

Homemade. Sally saw traces of flour and cinnamon and apple peelings not cleaned up yet. "How did you find the time to bake, lady?"

"I took the day off."

Sally noticed a difference in her realtor, her friend – a sparkle she hadn't seen a few weeks ago.

"Why Claudia Wilcox, pardon me for being intrusive, but I do believe you have a boyfriend."

Claudia paused and tilted her head. "Does it show?"

"You are radiant. Positively glowing and that doesn't come from new cosmetics. I know because since our kids moved out, Steve and I, well let's just say we have new, uh, vitality."

Grinning, Claudia held a finger to her lips as if to say it's our secret. "The guys are here. Shush them so they tread lightly. Kimmy needs a nap. A long one."

"Baby sleeping so the boss says for you to walk on tip toes, if possible." And the hunks from the gym carried large boxes, sniffing the air as they followed directions written in magic markers.

An hour later the moving truck left. The guys were on the back porch making quick work of pies. Sally and Steve looked around their new home. "Well, this was painless thanks to the kindness of strangers."

"Strangers no more, Steve. We've come to the right place."

The curly hair blond cutie awoke from her nap, to holler, "Uppy, now."

Sean appeared, pie crumbs on his mouth and picked up his baby girl. "Uppy, my girl." Expertly he laid her down and changed her diaper using wipes and sweet smelling lotion. "Time for food, my Kimmy. Come on, Mikey, big guy. Let's eat." They moved out to the porch with the young crowd where Sean took care of the children.

"Already we're a party house, Steve. I love it. I do wonder where Marlena is."

"When last seen, she was on two cell phones and had her computer going with fingers flying. Interesting combination of temperament and shared abilities."

"Let's unpack our bedroom stuff and bathroom things. By the way, did you notice the pretty couch is still here? And the back porch table and chairs? What's this all about?"

Puzzled and weary, Steve shrugged. "First the bedroom and bathroom. At least we'll be able to sleep, wash, all the good familiar, you know."

They climbed the stairs where it was quiet. Steve patted her bottom.

"Thanks, honey. I needed that and more when everyone is gone."

Two hours later, the house had emptied of helpers as the Atwoods put their belongings away. Together, they made the bed with new sheets and a comforter to match. Their respective dresser drawers were neatly organized and all the shampoo, conditioners, make-up and toothbrushes and toothpaste they'd ever need, purchased on sale at CVS before the big move, were in place.

Down the stairs they went, tired, hungry for one more look around before turning off the lights. The couch and matching chairs remained, pillows fluffed up. Baby toys all gone. Porch furniture still there. Back to the kitchen. Steve opened the fridge to find food, glorious food. A roasted chicken, baked lasagna, fresh vegetables in the tray and cheese, crisp apples and bananas on the counter.

"Do you recall the fairytale of the Elves and the Shoemaker?"

Steve shook his weary head. "Nope. Mom never read stories to me."

"Poor baby. If I remember correctly, elves came in the night and did all the work for the old shoemaker as he slept. It's like what happened today. We were prepared to move by ourselves knowing it was a big job and we arrived to find the elves ready to pitch in and make our job easy. Steve, I'm overwhelmed by what happened today. Once we're settled in, we'll find a way to give back to this wonderful community."

"You're right. Now let's have a bit of that lasagna and then we'll try out the new sheets to see if they work."

"What a romanticist you aren't."

He poured red wine while Sally heated two slices of Italian deliciousness. A toast with glasses raised, the Atwoods said, "To us." Chimes rang.

"It's nine o'clock. Who can that be? Everyone we know here left a long time ago."

"Look through the peep hole, Steve. You can't be too careful." She grabbed a knife from the carving set to be prepared for a stranger.

Steve opened the door. "Johnny. What a surprise and who's behind you? Oh, Tiffany. Come in. Sally, it's the kids."

Chapter 10

Sally warmed the rest of the lasagna while two forlorn newlyweds poured out their story.

"We're sorry to uh, burden you with our trouble, I mean problem, but my parents are out of town, like in Europe, right now and..."

"We're pregnant and Tiff's scared 'cause it's so soon and she blames me."

"Slow down, kids. Kick off your shoes and eat. The lasagna is delicious. Our realtor left this in the fridge so we wouldn't have to go shopping. Milk, juice, water?"

"Milk, please." Cheeks flushed, Tiffany held up her glass. "Thanks for being so Mom and Dad just when we needed you instead of hollering. I know we barged in at a busy time. Moving is crazy."

"We were lucky." Sally made them laugh relating the party, hunky friends to help and apple pies and babies.

"Babies here today? What a coincidence."

"I guess there aren't any coincidences, John. And we loved having little ones in our new house. For your information, I got pregnant with your sister, Lisa, right away. What a surprise. Your Dad was just starting with his first corporate job and we didn't know how we'd manage."

"But we did." Steve finished his wine and cleared the table. "John, help me unroll the sleeping bags since we don't have an extra bedroom set up. Then you both shower up and get a good night sleep. We'll talk more tomorrow morning."

"Thanks, Mom, for welcoming us. We've been arguing for a week. I wanted to run away. Stupid, I know."

Sally gazed at the worn out girl her son had married a few months ago. No longer the perfect bride in white satin with blond curly hair cascading around her bare shoulders. Now Tiffany wore Johnny's sweat shirt from college and baggy boy friend jeans from the GAP. She needed sleep, comfort and communication with her husband.

"You're just scared, honey. I promise it will work out. Have you seen a doctor?"

"No. I used the home pregnancy kit and almost fainted. Then I threw up."

A motherly hug from Sally calmed the thin frightened girl. "Okay. That's the next step but first get a good night's sleep and make up with your husband. It's not his fault, Tiffany. It takes two to create a new life. Did you pack an overnight bag?"

"Oh, it's in the car."

Together they walked outside, heard cicadas and hoot owls in the trees, the stars so close, Sally wanted to pluck them from the sky. She dragged the bag from the back seat, pictured a car seat in about eight months. A baby in the family. Mother-in-law and daughter-in-law bonded in the moonlight. All would be well.

The new house quieted after whispers from the room down the hall subsided and finally stopped. "Just when we thought it was safe to go into the water..."

"The doorbell rang or chimed or whatever..." Steve finished the thought. "Now what do we do?"

Sally spooned against the warmth of him under the new sheets and sighed. "In the morning, we make breakfast, do a bit of parenting and send them home to work it out."

"Easier said than done, sweetheart. They're not tough the way our generation was at the same age."

"They'll have to learn. We'll be here for them with a listening ear and years of experience."

"Hmm. Shall we celebrate our first night here?"

"You mean like this?" Sally pressed closer to her husband's body and felt him rise to the occasion.

"Starting just like that, baby. And quiet so our guests won't hear."

She giggled and the loving began. "Slip a pillow under here." Sally raised her hips and he did as requested. "Now come to Momma, come to Momma, do."

Down the hall in the guest room, with moonlight shining through shutters, Johnny and his bride grinned at each other. "I want us to be like them."

"It takes work to make a good marriage, Johnny. Are we ready?"

"You bet we are." He caressed her belly. "And if we have questions, my parents will have suggestions. We'll figure out the rest of it."

"Tomorrow we'll head back home. Thanks for insisting we come to River's Edge and for your amazing Mom and Dad."

"Do I smell coffee?" Sun streamed through painted white shutters they'd forgotten to close before going to bed. Birds tweeted, taking free breakfast from the feeder Sean must have filled the day before. Steve stretched and yawned. "I love the country."

"Must be the elves made coffee. I hope they're into scrambled eggs. I'm hungry. Brush your teeth and run down while I get dressed."

"You brush my teeth, woman."

She tossed a pillow at him, missed and giggled. It was the same pillow he slid under her hips last night. Steve picked it up, sniffed and knew what the giggle meant.

"Get over here, big guy. You can't breathe fire on the kids."

He grinned, did the deed , threw on sweats and a tee shirt and hurried down, sniffing all the way.

A happy couple sat at the table holding hands, restored after food and sleep and maybe a small dose of family counseling. Returned to former lustrous beauty, Tiffany looked radiant.

"Good morning. You're up early. Thanks for coffee. That's one job I won't have to do this day."

"I have to get back to work, Dad, but we appreciate you taking us in on one of the busiest times, moving day. Your new house is beautiful. I'm thinking you've got a long commute to New Jersey where corporate headquarters is and also Newark Airport since you travel so much."

Steve blew on hot coffee and took a gulp. "Son, I'm sad to say that Hiro-San decided to retire me a few weeks ago without further discussion. So I'm no longer employed after thirty years of steady work." He stirred his coffee, head bent as if a better answer floated in the mug.

Johnny almost knocked over his chair in the haste to get close to his Dad. He threw his strong protective arms around him.

"Damn. This bites the big one, Dad. What will you do now?"

Steve met his son's worried eyes. "Good question. No answer." He patted John's hand. "After we unpack, your Mom and I will job hunt. Poor planning has left us in this state. Keep this in mind. Work hard, save your money for your later years and don't be careless about investing. You're having a baby. Sean Adler is a financial planner at Trumbull Realtor. He's a bright young man who knows what's what. Next time you're here, make an appointment with him."

"What's this?" Sally danced into the kitchen, a bright smile on her face. "Your Dad sounds like he's on a soapbox preaching to the choir. I see by the worry on your faces he's told you he's unemployed. I say, not to worry. Steve Atwood is a man of many talents and we are survivors. Now hit the road and keep in touch. We want to know all about the baby."

After hugs and kisses, they waved the younger generation goodbye.

"Alone at last. Let's tackle the boxes and then, sweetheart," Sally grabbed hold of her husband's tee shirt, "we'll tackle each other."

Chapter 11

By late afternoon, the Atwoods locked the door of their new home and drove over to Trumbull Realtor. They'd decided since their generous new friend loved fresh flowers, they would buy some for her. Sally carried the flower arrangement of purple hyacinths, red roses and baby's breath in a tall ceramic vase bought at the Pick Two, Take One Flower Shop on Main Street.

Steve opened the door, his wife paraded in before him.

"And who is that bringing Spring into our establishment? How gorgeous. Some folks might say, "Oh, you shouldn't have." As for me, I say, "What took you so long? Thanks, you two. I bet you're weary after unpacking all those boxes. Sit you down. I made lemon squares and saved some for you. Sean packed a bunch to take home. He's still here." She tapped a button to summon her son.

"About the couch and..."

"Stop right there, Steve. Please accept them as a housewarming gift. My pleasure. Now how did your evening go?"

"You will not believe this but at about nine-thirty, just as we were warming slices of lasagna an elf left in the fridge, the doorbell rang. Our son and his bride showed up, bedraggled and sad in need of family to help sort out a tiny problem. Right, Steve?"

He shrugged his shoulders and munched on the finest lemon squares ever.

"She's pregnant." Claudia smiled and tapped her forehead to show off diagnostic power.

Steve almost choked on the powdery lemon square. "Bingo!"

They laughed, high-fived and then a disheveled Sean walked in. "You're pregnant, Sally?" More laughter and *heaven forbid* from all.

"So you're here because you're settled in and want to know what's next."

"Mindreader Sean at work." Claudia kissed his cheek. "Here are a few newspapers with job opportunities for you, Sally." He handed a small pack to her." I suggest you check on Cable TV stations. They're always searching for news reporters. I have connections with everyone. After you show me a sample of your writing, I'll judge who you should contact." He turned his attention to Steve. "How about you? Do you have any ideas of what you'd like to do now that you're a free man?"

"Nicely put, Sean. Free man. Instead of thrown under the bus old obsolete guy."

"No bitterness here. We seek positive energy for this to work. I have a project needing one more man and you may very well be the right guy."

Head nodding, Steve wiped crumbs from his five o'clock shadow. "Lay it on me, young master."

Sean grinned. "It's easy. Your deck at the old house is finished and needs spraying before the new buyers move in. I'll show you how to run the spray gun. The funny thing is the couple selected light yellow paint."

"Light yellow. Geez." Steve groaned. "That porch, I mean deck should be stained natural."

"Well, it's their deck now so who cares. Are you game? The pay is good. I provide gloves, coveralls, a cap. We go tomorrow."

"Okay. Are you driving?"

"Sure. We have an official truck. This is a side business for our Flip Houses. It can be very lucrative. And already we've flipped a lot of houses. I'll pick you up at six a.m. Bring lunch. For me, too. Some of that chicken sliced thin on whole wheat, salad on the side."

"Sean, that's an imposition."

"Heck no, Moms. That's why I bought the roaster and left it in their fridge. I knew Steve wanted work and this is perfect. Leaving early, I don't have to do the kids. Marlena will take care of day school stuff."

After saying goodbye, the Atwoods stopped at the local grocery shop to fill in with Sean's request. "He's dynamic, isn't he?" Sally carried one bag, Steve, the other.

"To say the least. We're in for an adventure, my dear."

"Yes, we are."

Bright and early Sean tapped on the truck's horn. Steve raced out, lunch packed, ready to go. "Bye, honey. Have a good day." Sally had to laugh. How often over the years did she call out to her children the same words.

In the quiet of the new house, she checked out the newspapers, circled possibilities and Googled the cable stations to see where she might fit in. Excited, she made lists to discuss with Sean and made sure her resume was good enough to inspire someone in charge to take a second glance.

She looked at her watch. An hour had passed and pictured the truck arriving at the old neighborhood. Steve, not in a suit and tie, but dressed in a coverall and cap ready to learn how to use a paint sprayer. She said a quick prayer he'd get it right. Handy man he never was. Yellow? Hoping he would spray only the deck, not the walkway, she changed into a running suit and headed out through the neighborhood on a clear sunny late Spring day.

"Hold the sprayer like this now that it's filled." Sean showed Steve the way, eager to get on with another house. "Then push the red button to activate and away you go, carefully. Don't stay in one place too long. Kind of wave the sprayer with care in long sweeps. Got it?"

"Uh, I think so." Goggles on, Steve squared his shoulders and began. At first it went well, he thought, and then everything turned to cursing. By then, Sean had driven away. Steve was alone with no one to guide him. *This isn't rocket science, you nitwit. Push the damn button and spray.* Losing control of the sprayer was the worst catastrophe. Suddenly the thing had a mind of its own. It bounced down the deck steps and sprayed the brick path to the house. Follow the yellow brick road, Steve hummed as he finally got control, refilled his evil weapon and finished the porch. *Not bad. I wonder what the big boss will say.* After trimming the new grass to remove the yellow, he found a board and with a black magic marker wrote, Welcome to Yellow Brick Road. Propped against a big rock, the sign had a happy appearance. If they had a sense of humor, they'd chuckle over this. If not, two words for them and they weren't Happy Birthday.

Neighbors passed by smiling and waving hi. Steve stripped out of his coveralls and washed in the kitchen, a stream of yellow paint rushing down the drain. He changed to a clean tee shirt and jeans, had lunch outside and hurried around to the front when the truck pulled up.

Sean climbed out, a big grin on his good looking face. "How'd it go, my friend?"

"We had our moments, Mr. Spraygun and me. Take a look before you say I'm fired.'"

They looked at Steve's handiwork as a not–so–handyman. Sean cracked up when he saw the brick walkway. He pounded Steve's aching shoulders. "Man, you've got it goin' on. This is the coolest. They'll love it. Now let's head home. We've both had a most productive day."

Steve snored all the way to River's Edge.

Sean glanced over at his friend with pride. *From corporate executive thirty years to handyman with imagination in one day. My kind of man. I think I'll adopt him.*

Chapter 12

"Look at you, honey." Sally led her tired husband to the mirror in the powder room. "I kind of like the yellow stripe effect that runs through your gray hair. Where oh where did that come from? The hair salon in New City?"

After a close look , Steve groaned. "The damn spraygun attacked me. It went ballistic. I couldn't turn it off and all of a sudden..." He glanced again. "It had a life of its own and, and, painted the brick walk."

"You mean the deck and the walk are yellow?"

"Uh huh."

Giggles began. The wet wash cloth did a good job erasing most of the paint. Every time the Atwoods checked out the progress, they laughed until Steve thought a shower for two might be the answer. Later, wrapped in a bath towel, Sally still had the giggles.

"So now you're a handyman?"

"Yup, kind of. In the learning phase but I can take classes or Sean will teach me. I like using my hands."

"I know, sweetheart. Oh how I know. And we did good for Johnny and Tiff, didn't we?"

"Absolutely and before long, a grandchild."

"So River's Edge is our home stretch, our happy ending."

In one quick drop of her towel, Sally stood before her mate.

She looked as good to him as the first time, on their honeymoon.

"This is just the beginning, babe. . .not the end."

Help Wanted

by

Charmaine Gordon

Dedication

To my publisher and friend, Kimberlee Williams.
Because you believed in me, I believed in me.
Here is my seventeenth story.
Are we having fun? You bet we are!

Acknowledgements

To my long time pal, Judy Audevard, I give thanks. I had an idea about bringing therapy dogs and their owners to a fictional town, River's Edge, and called the expert, Judy. As Director of Hudson Valley Paws for a Cause, Judy did what I call, Picture This. She sent me an email so powerful telling me her feelings the first time she and her friends went to West Point to visit wounded veterans, taking the therapy dogs with them. Chapter Eleven is real in so many ways.

Thank you, Pat, Susan and therapy dogs, Darla and Douglas, both Labs, and Jessie, a German Shepherd.

The title Help Wanted comes from the creative mind of Chelle Cordero, an author and good friend. Once again I have the pleasure of thanking you, Chelle.

And to you, dear readers, please enjoy Help Wanted. One day you may find your nest is empty and you want to spread your wings and fly.

Chapter 1

"Sally Atwood."

Sally jumped when she heard the receptionist call her name. She picked up the dropped briefcase and gathered spilled papers, embarrassed in front of all the young reporters waiting for an interview. Jerald Adams had the reputation as high man on the totem pole of local news. Also rumored to be a womanizer. So beware was the warning. *This is it, your first meeting. Make a good impression.*

She entered the office, smelled cigars and wrinkled her nose.

"Well hello, Sally Atwood. Have a seat and tell me why you wrinkled that pretty turned up nose? I guess you don't like the smell of cigars."

She sat deflated like a whipped pup knowing she'd gotten off to a bad start.

"I'm sorry it I offended you, Mr. Adams. I'm here to show you what I've accomplished so far and promise if, after you see my reporting ability, I'll get, uh, used to the scent." She pulled out a folder to hand across the desk.

His black hair pulled in a short pony tail came undone when the heavy set man threw his head back and laughed letting the folder drop. "Funny and pretty. A good combination." He rose and came around the desk, towering over the petite Sally.

"Get me an interview with Grace Trumbull at the Pet Emporium with her doing the special dog communication thing she's known for and you're hired, little lady."

"I'll be back before you know it and thanks so much, Mr. Adams."

Thrilled with possibilities, eager to be away from his innuendos, she gathered her folder, briefcase and bag and hurried out after a firm handshake that lingered too long.

"Just do it. Suck it up and go," Sally said to her image in the mirror. *Words guaranteed to encourage herself.* Dressed down in a white shirt tucked into dark blue tailored pants, at the last minute Sally tied a colorful silk scarf around her neck. She slung the worn leather bag over her shoulder packed with a new camcorder Steve gave her to celebrate the transition from homemaker to reporter. Head held high, Sally drove downtown to the Pet Emporium

The bell chimed a cheerful greeting when Sally entered into a chorus of barking dogs and handlers at work. A tall muscular man walked over.

"Hi I'm Scott Dwyer. Welcome to the Pet Emporium.

"I'm Sally Atwood. I'm a reporter. The cable station's chief Jerald Adams challenged me to get an interview with a prominent woman he calls the dog communicator." Sally breathed in and out and went on. "He called it an in-depth interview and if I'm able to speak with the famed Grace Trumbull, I've got the job."

Scott Dwyer laughed, covered his mouth and laughed harder while he steered Sally to a small alcove and closed the door. The noise subsided after the door closed. She smelled brownies, hot from the oven and the gurgle of tea from a pitcher pouring over ice. Her host set the beverages and a plate on a round wood table.

"Jerry's bark is worse than his bite. He's tough and has to be in the business, Sally. Welcome to River's Edge, by the way. Claudia Wilcox is a good friend. She said we'd meet you before long. So you're ready to get a job. Have you worked before?" He poured tea and tapped the brownie plate. "I make these every day. After smelling dogs and cats in soapy water, it's nice to have a home baked aroma in here."

She liked the casual way this man spoke with assurance and kindness, not just being nosy. "After raising three kids and being a stay-at-home mom for many years, it's time. I took some classes in communication, journalism and reporting. I do have a few credentials from work in Rockland County if you'd like to check them out."

"Please."

She handed him the dog eared folder, made a mental note to use a new one next time, if there was a next time, and took a bite out of the brownie. *Oh my God. The taste of chocolate so sweet, fat free, of course.* She grinned. *Yeah right. Calm down.* She restrained herself from the desire to inhale the entire piece even though it beckoned..

His blue eyes scanned current columns Sally wrote. "Good. I like your style. Warm and friendly, not pretentious. Wait a sec."

He left the room and in that brief moment, she checked her lipstick, brushed away telltale crumbs. True to his word, Scott returned in a flash just as Sally blotted fresh lipstick.

"You look just right, Sally. You're in luck. Grace is in a good mood. She says any friend of Claudia's is a friend of ours and right now she's in conference with a sad saluki."

"Saluki?"

"Yeah, they need gentle training, saluki companions and lots of exercise otherwise the owner should buy a different breed. So take care when you and Steve decide to get a dog or two. "

"You're getting ahead of us, Scott. First I need a job. Maybe then we'll talk about a pooch."

"About the interview, don't get too close. You have a camcorder?" She nodded and felt so professional. "Good. When I point to you, begin. The idea is to catch the intimate scene. Let's go."

Heart hammering with excitement, Sally walked behind Scott to the designated spot and watched, hand held the camera trained on a magnificent medium size dog. He pressed his nose against the cheek of a lean youthful woman, hair swept in a knot at the back of her neck, and the dog let out a low mournful sound. She stroked his head all the way down his back several times murmuring in his ear. They repeated the process over and over. Rubbing his nose against her fingers, a few laps like kisses with his tongue, the silent conversation continued. Grace nodded, listening and gave her full attention to the sleek graceful unhappy dog. When he lifted a paw to her face to pat as if saying thanks, Grace embraced the silky haired canine in need of comfort.

Sally, the observer, felt her own tears fall with the beauty of the moment. A quick blot with her new white shirt sleeve and the atmosphere changed. Abruptly Scott made the cut motion with his finger across his throat. Sally turned off the equipment and hurried to the alcove to wait. The owner of the sad saluki had arrived to discover the results. This had nothing to do with Sally's business here.

A breathless Grace entered the small room about ten minutes later. "There you are. Thanks for waiting. I refused to let Sammy go home with her until she buys another companion saluki to keep him company. He's sad and lonely just like a human. Salukis need companionship and lots of exercise. I warned her in the beginning, gave her the name of the best breeder nearby. I make no profit from the sale. This is for the good of the animal." She sighed. "I hope she takes my advice or she'll have to sue me for custody." Grace poured tea, munched on a brownie and smiled. "Now where do we start?"

Sally had to laugh. This dynamo of a woman defied Sally's expectation. Where to begin? At the beginning, of course, the way reporters do.

Camcorder on, she began. "You found River's Edge how, if it's not too personal."

Grace's big brown eyes focused on a middle distance and dimpled at the memory. "The kindness of strangers led me here and here I've stayed to open the Pet Emporium with Jim Trumbull. Fate guided me and I'm so grateful." Her working hands gestured to the building.

"And your gift. People call you the 'dog whisperer or communicator.' I watched you with the sad saluki and I could swear you understood each other."

Frowning, a few beats passed before Grace answered. Her face was a study of deep thought and Sally let the camcorder capture her mood.

"I call it a communication just as you and I are doing now. It's not a mystical talent as far as I'm concerned. I listen and get a sense of what's going on. We've never met before but I feel your anxiety. You need a job to establish yourself. Jerry Abrams waved a carrot in front of your nose by saying get an in-depth interview with the reclusive Grace Trumbull. Delete this part, please. I'm going to knock his socks off with this interview and you'll get the job. After that, Ms. Atwood, you're on your own and personally, I know you'll be great."

Fortune smiled when Sally checked the equipment to find she had batteries for at least another hour as she learned about Grace and the way she conducted business from day one. At the end of their time together they shook hands. Grace went back to work; Sally headed home happy to know she'd found another friend in River's Edge.

Chapter 2

Hmm. Something smells good, Sally thought and breathed in beef stew when she unlocked the door. Steve hummed in the kitchen, wrapped in an apron and nothing else. After so many years together she knew him almost too well. He had a plan obviously. Woo his wife with dinner and she'd be ready for romance.

"Hi. Did you get the in-depth interview with Grace Trumbull the big boss wanted? Taste this" Steve opened the cover of the crock pot and ladled a small portion of stew for Sally's approval.

"Yum. Perfection. Just what I needed. And I said you couldn't cook." She kicked off her shoes and wiggled her toes. "Yes, Steve. I did. Grace is wonderful and Honey, we must get a dog or two and soon. After dinner I'll run it for you. Tell me what you think should be trimmed. I need your advice. After all the presentations you've given, you have an eye for how a good show should look. And by the way, big guy, did I ever properly thank you for the camcorder? If not, tonight's the night."

"You're welcome. I hope it worked well with no glitches. Dogs? Well, maybe. First, the stew is ready. I found your old crock pot recipe book covered with drippings of dried food. I'll get a new one at the book shop in town and keep mine clean,"

Sally scoffed at the idea. "Wait 'til you've been preparing meals for years with noisy kids at... Oh. No more kids. You can cook in peace and have clean cook books plus be organized. What a luxury."

He kissed his wife and pulled loose the clip that held her curly blond hair in control. "You were always a great mom and home maker. It's my turn to pitch in. I'll put the temp on warm because I can't wait to see what you've accomplished today." Steve poured two glasses of red wine and brought out sliced Jarlsberg cheese and crackers on a plate. Sally darkened the room by pulling night shades down and closed the draperies. Excited for the first showing, she set up a pillow to balance the equipment.

Zooming in on the first shot, the elegant saluki pressed his nose to Grace Trumbull's cheek in an intimate moment. Steve inhaled sharply and let his breath exhale low and slow as he watched the silent story unfold. Fifteen minutes of human and animal memorable contact followed by an animated brisk woman, who spoke with humor and knowledge about her business, the Pet Emporium and what it means to her.

"Bravo, Sally. You've done it. My advice is to trim just a bit of the silent part. Keep it emotional enough and then cut to Grace. The transition will be startling and exciting. If this local community cable station doesn't hire you, there are others. I'm so proud of my wife."

Beaming, the Atwood's toasted to Sally's project with wine. On a high, she removed her silk scarf and dropped it to the couch. Next, the white shirt somehow came unbuttoned followed by a shimmy of her hips as dark blue pants slipped to the carpet.

"Here or upstairs?"

"Flip a coin, big guy."

"No money, no pockets. Just me in my cooking apron."

Sally embraced her big bear of a man. "Bring the wine. I'll carry the cheese plate. Hot tub and we'll see what happens next."

They had a very late supper that wonderful night, one of many as they continued to celebrate life alone in their empty nest.

Too nervous for breakfast the next morning, Sally dressed with care in a gray tailored suit and pink silk blouse. She decided to add a scarf for a signature to her outfits from now on.

Steve ran out, lunch box packed for an indoor house painting job. "See you later, Sweetheart, knock his socks off."

Stay at home no more, old girl. She sang, "Don't Stop Thinking about Tomorrow—yesterday's gone, yeah yesterday's gone." "Tomorrow, here I come." Her smile didn't waver until she saw the big sign, River's Edge Community Cable appear. "Knock his socks off" came back to her spoken first by Grace Trumbull and then last night and again this morning by the man who loved her." *Okay, Jerald Adams, be prepared because I'm going to do just that. God, I hope he's wearing socks.*

"Sally Atwood to see Mr. Adams."

The same receptionist checked the appointment book and with a sour look meant to pierce a heart, glowered at Sally. "You don't have an appointment."

Using her authoritarian voice, Sally said, "Mr. Adams requested that I come in as soon as possible since I have fulfilled his assignment to obtain the in-depth interview with Ms. Grace Trumbull. I have it right here." She patted her trusty equipment bag.

"Oh. Just a minute. " Out and in, she returned, a smug look on her face. "Mr. Adams said he's not interested in such an interview and thanks you for your time."

The words for Dirty Dancing popped into Sally's mind. "Nobody puts baby in the corner." What kind of treatment is that to dish out after sending her to take up Grace Trumbull's time, let alone waste her time? Sally Atwood stormed through the door, eyes blazing.

The large imposing man sat, feet crossed at the ankles up on his desk, puffing on a cigar, king of a small kingdom. His eyes widened at Sally's unexpected intrusion. Before he had time to shout, she went into a controlled tirade.

"In good faith, I followed your assignment with a promise for a job. I fulfilled my part and now I've wasted an important member of River's Edge Counsel's time. Ms. Trumbull was gracious in granting me an interview. This won't go unnoticed, I can assure you." Sally spun on her heels and left Jerald Adam's office.

In the car, she began to shiver. *How did she ever have the audacity to do...and say...Oh my God! And once spoken, words can't be taken back. Oh no. She's ruined her reputation in the business before she even got a toe hold. What to do next? Her product was perfect and she had no one to show it to. Then she recalled a conversation with Sean Adler when they first moved in. He said he knew everyone.* She drove to Trumbull Realtor and hoped the handsome young man was there.

Claudia Wilcox opened welcoming arms when Sally walked in.

"It's so good to see you. What's up? You're troubled."

"Your sixth sense is at work, Claudia." Sally explained the situation after sipping tea and knocking off two coconut cookies.

"That egotistical bastard. It's good you told him off. Let's see the interview. Grace never granted one before. You obviously made a fine impression." Claudia gathered a pitcher of tea and cookies and left word not to be disturbed with her receptionist. "Let's go in my inner office. I'll call Sean. He'll want to see your work."

Feeling comfortable with friends, Sally set up the camcorder she'd taught herself to use. Sean bounced in like a big kid, a wide smile on his face.

"Show us what you've got, lady."

Silence in the room until the end and then a standing ovation. "Sally, this is as professional an interview as I've seen in a long time. I had tears when Grace and the dog communicated." Sean paced the room. "So Jerry Adams acted like a big shot without looking at your interview. Well he's a fool acting like that. River's Edge is a small fish in the big pond of social media. I'm going to call some people I know and see if they'd be interested in your work. Meanwhile, don't let this get you down. There's a small project you can do for our new company, Flip Houses, with the white truck Steve's been driving."

Sally's mind took hold of the idea. Flippin' Houses...a great idea. Don't just sit; Flip!

She grabbed a drawing pad from Claudia's desk and creative juices flowed. Sean crouched behind her and grinned. "Moms, check this out. We've got a winner. And that's your first thought, Sally. Hmm. Only terrific and funny."

"Zippity do da day, Flip your house the Trumbull Realtor Way" and Don't start snippin'; just get Flipin'. Call-----" Sally cracked up. "That's for starters. I don't know where it came from but here we are. And please don't compliment me too much. I'm uh, not used to too much praise. Remember, I've been a homemaker for thirty five years."

"Time to spread your wings, lady. I'll get on this right away." Sean jumped to his long legs and almost danced out of the office.

"My son likes you, Sally. He admires the way you didn't let Jerry Adams get you down. Mr. Adams will be sorry.

You've got a career ahead of you and you're funny. That's a plus. Now go home and get comfortable. There's work to be done. I'm sure Sean will be calling before too long. How about dinner with us later this week?"

"Are you referring to your beau? From the glow on your face, I'm assuming all is well."

"Assume all you want, my friend. Yes, we're doing just fine. How about Thursday evening at seven, my home."

"Cool. See you then unless business calls and I'll see you sooner."

Sally sang all the way home thinking about tomorrow. A day so filled with promise turned out to be a bonanza by the happy end.

Chapter 3

Business clothes hung up, Sally changed into running shorts and a Tee shirt. She didn't want to miss fresh air and busy with getting settled in the new house, she hadn't checked out the winding roads in the community. Sneakers tied, she headed out the door to quick walk. Claudia's plantings were so pretty. The flagstone path had a border of geraniums blooming already. Yellow, dark red, white all mixed together made quite a show. The best thing is they grow back. Perennials. Her favorites. She almost skipped then remembered there were no kids around as an excuse in this adult community. The house they bought, Claudia's house, suited them just fine.

Two houses down, a neighbor waved. Sally stopped to say hi and admire her plants.

"Hi, I'm Doris Carbone, retired nurse and you're Sally Atwood, the newbie reporter."

"How in the world do you know my name and what I'm trying to do?"

"River's Edge is a small town. The word is out, Sally. You were seen at the Pet Emporium this morning."

Sally had to laugh. "Doris, what did I wear?" They both laughed.

"I wasn't paying attention but," she moved closer, "where did you get that scarf? I love flowered silk to perk up whatever you wear. But as I said, I didn't peek. Valerie told me."

"Valerie?"

"Here she comes. Former principal of a high school. She's a doll with a tough exterior. Hi Val. Meet Sally."

"So how's Grace?"

By now the laughter was contagious. Sally had walked three houses down and already she'd met two terrific funny women. *There must be more*, she thought.

"I hope you play tennis or something. We just lost a fourth. Our dear pal Sonia moved to Florida. Damn Sidney. He wanted the beach and shuffleboard, the old fumph. She'll be bored. We've been searching for an interesting new neighbor and you, Sally Atwood, are it." Valerie patted the newcomer on the back.

"I'm uh, flattered but I'm just beginning a new career and..."

"We won't hold that against you. You're spreading your wings later in life but remember, whenever you do, it's the right time. So we'll be your support system."

The tough side did blend with the kind side of Valerie. The walk around the community had turned out to be providential. Friends. It seemed like River's Edge attracted a whole bunch of them.

"You mentioned a fourth in your gang. I mean group or club." Again she'd provoked them into a burst of laughter. "What? I don't mean to offend anyone but what do you call yourselves?"

Doris wiped her eyes. "We're The Silver Belles."

The name spun around in Sally's creative mind. "Oh, I do love the name. And what specifically do you do? Do you do. God, how dumb. It sounds like doodoo." More chuckles.

"Sally's a keeper." Valerie's deep voice said. She coughed. "Pardon. Former smoker but the cough lingers on."

"Try Claritin. Maybe it's an allergy thingy."

"See what I mean, Doris?"

"I do. As to what we do do" Doris stifled a laugh, "We entertain at the Veteran's hospital once a month by dancing and bringing in healthy snacks."

"Dancing? Like a routine?"

"Sometimes. You'll see. And we play tennis, gossip, do good works. We make sure our community stays honorable and clean; a place to be proud of."

"Oh. Well, it keeps you off the streets and out of mischief, I guess. From what I've seen, the neighborhood is beautiful, kept up so neat."

"Thanks to Valerie. She's on the committee for beautification and catching up on who's up to no good. That's Val's specialty."

"Hey,Teresa." Doris flagged down a slim woman with a long gray braid flying behind as she slowed her fancy bike to a stop. They all reached out to steady both the bike and the woman as she climbed off and caught her breath.

Valerie barked out another cough. Sally, her mother's instinct in full blossom, reminded herself to bring a little white pill for Valerie to try. It had cured her allergy symptoms and she took one a day.

"I thought, I know, Dr. Feel Good said to lay off the bike for two weeks until you get all your strength back."

"That he did and so much more. And this must be Sally Atwood. Someone please open the little pack and give me a drink." Val pulled out a small bottle of Chardonnay and held it up for all to see.

"Detention for you, young lady." She looked in again to find a small bottle of energy drink. Scanning the ingredients, she nodded. "Okay." And opened the bottle to place it into her friend's shaking hand. "Come sit a while. Enjoy the birds and the flowers before the snow flies."

Color came back to Teresa's cheeks. Her eyes closed and Doris covered her with a big beach towel. Sally thought, *everyone has a story. All I did was go for a walk and here I am in the midst of a group of women who want to know more about me. The Silver Belles has a lovely ring to it.*

"I feel like I'm intruding. Teresa is recovering from an illness or trauma and you both are good friends in time of need. I'm a stranger and yet you've opened your arms to me. I'm over whelmed."

Doris hugged her. "Count yourself in, Sally. Right now Valerie and I will call Teresa's doctor. Nosy neighbor's, you know. If you're free tomorrow about noon, call and we'll have a meet. The four of us. The Silver Belles." She scribbled her phone number down including Valerie's and Sally continued on her fast walk through the winding roads of her new community. When she returned to Doris's house, pill in a small envelope, no one answered the doorbell. The only thing left to reassure Sally it wasn't a dream was the new bicycle that leaned against the garage. Probably she'd keep the allergy pill for herself. *Don't mother everyone.* A suggestion was all Val needed.

At her desk, she used photo shop to write slogans about flippin' in different fonts. Working fast, ideas continued to flow, Sally focused on nothing else. Like a horse with blinders on, she followed her thoughts and page after page rolled out. She'd have a lot to show Sean. The sky darkened, the front door opened and Steve called out his usual greeting, "Honey, I'm home. What's for dinner?" Now it was just a joke since they both had goals and shared chores including dinners.

She heard working boots drop to the floor. Moans and groans as he stripped off work clothes in the laundry room. *Good boy*, she thought. *Only took him thirty five years.* After rereading every page and checking them twice, Sally printed three copies and gave herself a mental pat on the back.

The big bear sat in the kitchen drinking a cool one wearing nothing but jockey shorts. She kissed her sweetheart. "How was your day? Did you paint a yellow brick road for this house?"

"No. This was an inside job. I go back tomorrow. Man, she loves weird colors and wants sponge painting in two rooms. It's okay by me. There's more money involved but I'm too tired to cook so I brought Chinese take-out for us. Hope you don't mind, honey. And no fooling around tonight. I need my beauty sleep."

Sally couldn't help it. She climbed on his lap and kissed him a few more times. How adorable to bring food home and make fun of physical work. Steve never came home happy and high spirited after years in the corporate world. Moving on was good for both of them.

"Take a shower while I set the table and share my adventures."

"Shower with me and we'll share our own adventure."

"Here's a deal. Eat in your jockey shorts and then we'll shower. We're both hungry."

Compromise is always a good thing in marriage. Words of wisdom from mother taught years before.

Chapter 4

Refreshed after dinner, shower and romance, eyes half closed Steve insisted Sally tell the outcome with the honcho of the cable company.

"Honey, it's a long story and I don't want to keep you up listening to me."

"Speak to me, baby." His words mumbled with approaching sleep.

What could she do? So she spilled the beans about Jerry Adams attitude turning her away without a glance and how she tore into the pompous ass and left.

Her husband bolted upright, eyes alert. And Sally broke down crying. She finished with, "And I drove to Claudia and Sean and they gave me a standing ovation and..."

"So you spoke for yourself and there are possibilities." He relaxed enough to fade into the seductive call of sleep.

"Yes, my love" She kissed his eyelids. "More tomorrow. Tune in to watch your wifey spread her wings."

6 a.m. *Buzzzzzzz.* The noisy alarm went off. Dressed in painter's coveralls, Steve hurried to the bedroom to stop the racket before Sally woke up. No problem. Running water in the bathroom gave him the big clue. Before his wife came out, he'd have coffee ready. Lunch box filled and ready to go, Steve sat eating scrambled eggs and toast. No apple dumplings in months. His wife seduced him with food so they'd check out River's Edge, small town she'd read about. He gazed around the cheerful house, smaller and more manageable than the old one. Just right. One glance at his watch and he headed for the door.

"Sally, I left bills on top of the check book in the office. Since I'm working, you take over the job of bill paying. Have a nice day, honey."

Too late she ran down the stairs to catch him. The truck drove off and turned the corner gone for the rest of the day.

"What the hell?" In a fury over the orders and attitude that she had nothing else to do but clean house and pay bills to add to chores even though he appreciated her new found talent, Sally stomped around the kitchen. Into the sink went the frying pan with remnants of scrambled eggs. Crumbs from toast were left on the table. Rice Chex and blueberries were enough for her. Finished, she gathered the Flippin' advertising campaign in an artist 's folder and head held high, she got ready to leave.

The phone rang. *What a dope. Only seven thirty a.m. and where in the world was she going,* she thought *and who calls so early in the morning? Steve to apologize? Uh, no.*

"Grace Trumbull, here, Sally. Sorry to call so early. Scott and I heard that Jerry at the Cable company was rude and didn't even look at our interview. We're furious and have a plan. Do you have time to meet for breakfast at the diner in about half an hour?"

"Good morning, Grace. I'd love to meet you at eight. See you then." Sally cast an eye at her empty cereal bowl and shrugged. *This day will be great with friends and plans.* Up the stairs she ran to add some make-up and change her clothes. *A working woman has to look spiffy. Who gives a flying fuffa to bills when she's about to spread her wings.* She softened. Tonight, after dinner, she'd help Steve with the bills. Maybe file the statements in an orderly way as he wrote the checks, or something. Teamwork. Not one person barking orders for the other to follow. And thinking of barking, Sally made a mental note to ask about the fate of the sad saluki.

The aroma of sizzling bacon on Main Street guided Sally to Molly's Home Cooking Diner. Grace and Scott waved her over to the corner booth. Their smiles made her feel right at home like grabbing a quick bite just because.

"What's your pleasure, Sally? Waffles with blueberries are exceptional." Scott offered her a taste of his dripping with syrup. Automatically Sally opened her mouth like a baby bird and chewed the morsel.

She clutched her heart. "Yes, yes, yes."

"Scott, does this remind you of the movie When Harry Met Sally in the diner."

"Orgiastic, isn't she?"

"Yes, yes, yes."

The three of them laughed so hard, Molly hurried over to join in the fun and take the order.

"I'll get what he's having." Another line from the movie and more giggles until they settled down.

Scott 's face changed as if business time had arrived. " I'm a police officer retired with the K-9 Unit. My dog is King, a German Shepherd, well known for our team work in criminal apprehension, drugs and a lot more. The point is, King and I were on a popular Rockland County Cable station many times. So," and he stopped to drink hot coffee and exchange a glance with Grace, "I called my connection there and with Grace's permission, told him about the taped interview. They're always looking for interesting stories; we know this is exceptional. Our plan is for you to drive down with me and show him the tape. Today. How 'bout that and why not?"

Sally gulped air. "Oh, I'm blown away. What time and what'll I wear?"

"Scott, is she our kind of gal or what? I like what you're wearing right now. Your casual look in dark jeans and a white shirt with the silk scarf around your neck is perfect. We're not in the big city, after all. Scott, when is Lance available?"

"Between ten and eleven this morning. I'll call to confirm. How about you, Sally? You'll have to go home for the interview unless your bag is still in the car."

"As a matter of fact, it is in the car." Coffee grown cold , she shook her head when Molly came by for seconds. "I've been meaning to ask about Sammy, the sad Saluki. How is he?"

Grace brightened. "The owner gave up. We've got him right now and he's calmed down and plays with King. Might you and Steve consider adopting him and if so, you know you'd have to buy another Saluki as a companion."

"I Googled the breed. They're expensive even if you have an uncle in the business. If I start making money on my own, I'd definitely talk it over with Steve." She picked at the waffle. "Sean and Claudia have a side business, called Flipping Houses. I'm doing an ad campaign for them."

"Sounds interesting. Let us know how it works. Pet Emporium could use a boost in customers."

"More about this later. We better hit the road, Scott."

Too nervous and excited to finish the waffle, Sally hurried to the restroom.

"What a dynamic woman. I like her a lot. She reminds me of me when I first came to River's Edge. Nineteen, pregnant, determined to make something of myself. And here's a late bloomer in her fifties with all the energy of a girl, creative juices just beginning to flow."

Scott held his wife in his powerful arms to kiss her with a passion to tingle her lips." If only, Grace. How often I think those two words. And we finally connected with our daughter and twin grand children, a terrific son-in-law happy together. My heart hurts for the loss of all the years."

"Hold that for later, love. Call to let me know what Lance has to say. If he wants me in person to be on the show, I promise, I'll do it."

They beat the rush of traffic and made it to the studio by nine forty five. Sally recognized the neighborhood on the outskirts of Suffern, a short distance from the railroad tracks. The plain gray building had a big sign, The Best of Rockland Cable. Someone had planted multi-colored petunias and yellow chrysanthemums all around the base sprucing up the drab area. About ten dusty cars were parallel parked close-by and one shiny red Ferrari.

"Grab your equipment bag and let's find Lance. Are you cool?"

"Not as cool as you but I'll try." They strode in; Sally tried to keep up with Scott's long footsteps.

"Hey, Scott." A young woman, dark rimmed glasses perched on her nose, broke into a big smile when they opened the door.

"Betty Ann, I thought you'd be in NYC big time by now. We have an appointment to see Lance. This is Sally Atwood. She's a reporter superb from River's Edge. Betty Ann meet Sally."

The women shook hands and they were buzzed into an elaborate studio with more cameras and fancy equipment that made Sally feel like small potatoes with what she'd brought. Lots' of activity went on yet when the crew saw Scott, they hustled over to slap him on the back and shake hands. A couple of women were in the room. They also ran over with hugs and kisses for the retired hero cop. The sea parted as the boss, a tall slim middle aged man hurried over.

Sally thought, *this must be Lance. What a change from Jerry Adams.*

"Good to see you, Scott and this is Sally Atwood. Hello. Let's see what you've got."

No small talk. Strictly business. She admired the approach. Her battered leather briefcase zipper almost stuck but she pulled it free and removed the camcorder. Without a word, she set it up, asked for lights out and action. Silence in the room. So focused on what she had done, Sally missed a few sobs and sharp intakes of breath. Twenty minutes later, The End. Lights up. Not a word was spoken. No standing ovation until... applause.

"Gang, remember what you've just seen. Sally Atwood captured a moment and squeezed your heart." He narrowed his deep blue eyes and gazed at her. "Where did you study, Ms. Atwood?"

"Just a class at night here and there. I never had time to do much. Never..."

"It's in your heart. Creative juice flows through your body and now you let it run. I'm overwhelmed with your talent. Scott, both of you please come to my office and let's talk business."

Sally packed her bag and followed Scott through a long hallway to a bright flower filled room. She made herself comfortable as the boss suggested, in a tweed visitor's chair. Automatically, Sally kicked off her heels to wiggle her toes.

Scott watched with a smile on his face and said nothing. They were there to conduct business. Lance Jordan, a long time associate through the cable connection, obviously liked Sally and had plans for her.

The tall imposing man stared hard at Sally from his perch at the edge of the wide desk. Her breath hitched at his intense gaze.

"Ms. Atwood, here comes one of the greatest lines from The Godfather. Can you guess what it is?"

Laughter from Scott as he sat back and observed his friend in action.

"You're putting me on."

"Why would I want to wear a girl?"

Jumping up, Scott shook his head. "This is like watching an old comedy routine, you two. So you're making

Sally an offer she can't refuse, right? Get to the point, Lance. We have a long ride back to River's Edge. Grace expects me at The Pet Emporium and Sally has something going on with Sean Adler."

Lance scowled. "With Ms. Atwood's permission, I prefer discussing business in private. My driver will take you home before too long once we hammer out the particulars of an agreement."

"It's your call, Sally."

"Hmm. It might take time to hammer," she giggled, "sorry, your words referring to business tickled me unaccustomed as I am to transacting agreements regarding my work. I don't have an appointment with Sean today although I did finish an advertising layout for him." She took a few deep breaths. "Wow. Talking business takes a lot of words, doesn't it? So Scott, thanks to you and Grace I'm here and Lance will send me home when we're finished. Uh, soon."

After shaking hands all around, Scott left and suddenly the fragrance of flowers filled the room. *What in the world happens next,* Sally wondered.

Moving fast, the lanky graceful man sat next to Sally in the lush chair Scott just vacated.

"Your work impresses me. For a first timer, you have a gift for sincerity, a way of bringing out the best in people." He touched her cheek. "Grown women have experience in life with handling husbands, children, friends and everyone you come in contact with. I bet you know the checkers at the super market, tellers at the bank and you have a genuine smile for everyone." She opened her mouth to speak. Lance touched her lips.

"Young women focus on their appearance. They're like un-ripened fruit, not ready yet. But you, Sally Atwood, I want you," he paused, "on my staff to interview politicians, celebrities, distressed citizens and whatever else comes up. For each job, I'm prepared to pay you one thousand dollars."

Speechless, all Sally did was form an O with her mouth. *Am I dreaming? Did he say one thou? Yes he did.*

She covered her inner hysteria as if another day, another offer of big bucks. "Okay, so you'll draw up a contract for how long? A month, six months, a year?"

The mood changed in the room. Serious business was about to be transacted.

196

"If you agree, we'll begin with six months. You'll have a lawyer to protect your interest and approve the validity of the contract. If other offers for your talent come in, I will have first refusal."

Head buzzing with possibilities, Sally was upfront. "I'm designing an advertising campaign for Trumbull Realtors. It's a funny take on Flipping Houses. They haven't seen the presentation yet. "

Lance shrugged. "That has nothing to do with interviews." A glance at his gold Rolex and a smile lit his face. "Do you have time for lunch before leaving for River's Edge? I'm game if you are."

"Talking contracts and money whets my appetite. Let's go."

Chapter 5

The red Ferrari gave not only a smooth ride but elicited head turning glances along the way. Sally recognized areas she'd traveled over the many years living in Rockland County and then they were on Route 303 pulling in to El Mario, a place she and Steve had never been to.

"This is strictly business." She adjusted the flowered silk scarf around her neck that had twisted on the ride. "I, uh, well, I've never had lunch or dinner with anyone other than Steve, my husband, my three children, Mom and Dad, friends and..."

"Say no more. I get the picture." He covered her small hand with his manly strong hand. "You've had a sheltered life and you're definitely not a worldly woman." He parked in the back. "That's another charming aspect of you. Silver requires buffing to bring out the patina lying below the surface."

Greeted at the door by a well dressed young man with a handshake and a jock type of back slap, Lance requested a table in the garden. He guided Sally, holding her hand through a winding path outside.

This is crazy, she thought. *Run, don't walk. He's too sophisticated for you and who needs the job? You do. You want it. So shut up and listen. Above all, say NO! to anything that doesn't have to do with business. And what does silver and patina have to do with me. Smooth talker. Oh yeah.* Then Lance opened the glass door to a garden right out of a guide picture book to Italy.

"Oh," is all Sally said and she caught her breath. "An olive tree. No three olive trees." She grabbed Lance's hand, too excited to think about the intimate gesture, and pointed to the large tree and two smaller ones toward the back with a narrow stream running through ending in a fountain. Many statues aged through years of exposure to the element were placed among flowers of the season. Flat stones layered in tiers separated the various flower beds.

"Years ago Steve and I were in Italy and saw gardens exactly like this. I wonder who designed it"

"The Grandfather. When they built El Mario, he wanted a replica of his home in Palermo so he worked with his hands and made it come true. The specialty at lunch is antipasto. Does that please you? If so, we can share."

"Yes, oh yes. God, I feel like a kid sitting in this gorgeous garden about to dine on antipasto. Is the young man who greeted you a family member?"

"Family business is what makes the place so fine. Yes. Someday he'll own El Mario. Meanwhile he's the only son and grandson. There are several beautiful daughters but of course, the men come first in their culture."

"I'd like to meet the Poppa. Is he here?"

"Of course. After we lunch and before his nap, I'll ask for an audience."

Lance Jordan makes things happen. A man of action. Am I way out of my league or what?

The aroma of antipasto arrived before the waiter brought the beautiful platter to the table with service for two.

"Do you know what the word antipasto means?"

"If this is a test, I pass with flying colors. It means 'before the meal' but Lance, I'm full just looking at this display of Italian wonder."

"Then let's sample these wonders, as you refer to them."

Sally searched for a large serving spoon or fork. None to be seen so she dug in, tasting, chewing bits of pepperoni and black olives while murmuring hmm, so good and yum. "The mozzarella is made right here in the kitchen. I just know it."

"You're right. I've had the pleasure of watching the kitchen staff at work. They've even fed me scraps."

She used the napkin to blot a touch of olive oil on her lips. "Did you ever do an in-depth interview with the owner and follow the chefs at work?"

"Sally," he beamed at her, "that's your next assignment. I'll ask permission from the chief. It would be a great promo op for them and you, with your knack for drawing people out, will be in charge. No hand held cameras and little recorders. You'll have techies to work with." Popping a slice

200

of pepperoni in this mouth, Lance sat back satisfied as if he'd just conquered the world.

"Wait a minute. Wait just a darn minute, boss. The ink isn't dry on our contract and you're ready to move on with another job?"

"Of course. Now hurry up and finish unless you want a doggy bag to take home."

They examined what was left on the platter. One lonely artichoke heart and some chopped Romaine leaves. Sally sliced the artichoke in half and forked into her mouth leaving the other half for Lance. He picked it up with his fingers and placed it in her mouth before she could protest. Then in a casual manner, he licked his fingers and rose.

In a hurry to leave the romantic setting, Sally gazed once again at the garden. Hummingbirds sang their tune sucking nectar from a Hyacinth bush. Reluctantly she turned and bumped into Lance standing behind her.

"Beautiful, isn't it?"

"Thanks for bringing me here. It's a real treat. I look toward to a sparkling interview incorporating all the old country family charm."

They headed up the Palisade Parkway toward River's Edge. No Mother's voice on his GPS. She smiled to herself recalling Steve behind the wheel, unwilling to look at homes. Months have gone by and here she is, the housewife with a real career making money all of a sudden. Steve's learned to help out and even cook and he has a whole new job. No suits but he's happy painting houses, working with his hands.

"You're smiling, Sally. Tell me what's on your mind."

The glass of wine with lunch loosened her tongue and she spilled. "We moved up here a few months ago and I'm thinking what a difference it's made in our life together. Steve was an executive with a major Japanese Company for many years and they let him go without warning. One day he went to work. The head honcho called him in and gave him walking papers. Later, Steve said it was time and a very good package so we looked for a house, new work and here we are." She sighed. "I'm actually a working woman after years of being a slave homemaker." She turned to Lance. "Thanks for this opportunity to spread my wings. That's how I feel. Caged and now set free. I will enjoy the excitement of working for your company. And the money. Very generous of you, Lance." Approaching the second light on Main Street , Sally pointed to The Pet Emporium across the street. "Look quick. Scott and Grace built that from the ground up, I think. I'll have to ask her."

"Calm down, my excitable one. We're at a green light and I'm moving on. I will definitely stop there after I take you home."

Sally sat back, excitement stifled for the moment and wondered why she felt like a kid who just won the big prize.

"The air is sweet up here and we're not that far from Rockland County. And is that a waterfall I hear?"

"Yes. It's a never ending wonder for anyone who visits. Have you heard about the River's Edge Restaurant...Oh, Lance, slow down and turn right at the next light and follow the winding road to Castle Atwood."

Steve's work truck was parked in the driveway, door opened, Steve in paint-splattered coveralls bent over searching for something. He lifted his head, knocking off his painter's cap, obviously to see who was in the red Ferrari blocking his way when he was about to leave.

"Hi honey. What brings you home so early? This is Lance Jordan. Scott drove me down to Lance's cable station. Lance offered me a contract and now, I'm a real working woman."

"I'd shake hands but mine aren't clean right now. Sounds like good news, Sally but I have to finish today's job so please move your car, uh, Lance." And after a fast awkward minute, Steve was gone.

Still bright and perky, Sally tucked the old equipment bag over her shoulder and hurried to open the front door. She realized this would be another adjustment in her life. *Call it role reversal or whatever. Just another marital hurdle to work out.*

"Your husband is annoyed, to use the term loosely."

"No biggie. I believe marriage is one long conversation. He'll get used to the change in our relationship."

Lance rocked back and forth on his fancy boots and began to pace around the main floor of the Atwood domain. "Nice digs you've got here. The best word to describe it is..." They both said cozy at the same time and laughed.

"After the warm greeting Steve offered, I appreciate the compliment."

"As you said, no biggie. You show up in a cool car with a stranger and he's in work clothes. It's got to be a bummer."

"Adjustments. Always adjustment in a marriage and now the biggest one awaits my dear husband."

A few strides and Lance stood closer, too close for her comfort. "I'm reinventing myself. I'm the same but different in many ways."

"Let me count the ways." Lance trailed a finger down her back.

"Are you married?"

Was that a grimace or a painful shadow across his face, she wondered. He didn't answer.

"On that happy note, I must leave. I'll be in touch, Sally Atwood, very soon, with a contract ready for you to sign plus your next assignment." His lips brushed hers and he left; the click of the closing door echoed in her ears.

In a daze, she wandered around the house in circles, changing clothes as she remembered something she'd read a long time ago. Her head ached. In the office there were a ton of books stacked to the ceiling. She used a stepstool to reach the top shelf in order to skim the titles. There, tucked into a corner, was the book about the stages of women's growth. With effort, she pried it from the tight place, giggling to see dust rise when it hit the carpet.

Curled up in the comfortable old leather chair, Sally searched for the chapter she had to read to understand what happened with Lance Jordan today and why he'd be attracted to a middle aged woman.

She read: **The middle years woman is just coming into her own, blossoming after years of caring for her family instead of the focus turning inward on herself. What does she want from life? Is she content to stay at home and be the caring wife and homemaker or does she choose to go out in the world to follow a dream of being an artist, a writer, an actor? The options are wide open. Look in the mirror, dear lady. There is a depth to you now from life experience. Have you noticed men swivel their heads when you pass by to look at you lately? Do you wonder why? The answer is pheromones. You have a scent about you and I'm not referring to perfume. This comes from personal sex with your mate. You** are comfortable and other men feel it. They want it. They want you.

Of course, this is an exaggeration. Also it's an alert. Look your best even when you go to the grocery store and see how many heads turn in your direction. Write to me, dear readers. Let me know what's going on in your mid years.

Sally checked the date of publication. Hmm. Twenty years ago. Her experience today held true. An attractive important man came on to her in a big way. Even that womanizer fool, Jerald Adams was ready to jump her middle aged bones. And she had been faithful to Steve for thirty-five years, never thinking about another man. But Lance stirred something inside her and she felt as if she'd cheated on her husband just with a thought. The book, wiped clean, had a new place on the lowest shelf toward the end. Just in case.

Time for a hot shower and back to work on possibilities for a new interview. Memories of the El Mario garden drifted through her mind; three olive trees, the stream, antipasto. Yes. Begin at the beginning. Grandfather, proud in the kitchen, in charge of several chefs in command like a maestro but instead of a baton, he waves a wooden spoon. The young grandson, heir to the business followed by dining in the garden to get the full impact of the beauty of an Italian success story.

Wrapped in a towel, she hurried to the office and began to elaborate on the story, scene by scene. The FAX arrived in the tray. Pulse racing, Sally grabbed her glasses and read.

"What an extraordinary pleasure meeting with you today, Sally. I stopped to thank Scott and Grace at the Pet Emporium for introducing us. Attached is the six month contract. Have your lawyer check it out and approve. Sign and return. I look forward to working with you very soon."

Lance Jordan

This required a call to Claudia. She had said she'd call in a marker from a lawyer friend in town. Hands trembling she fumbled the phone after punching the wrong number. *Calm down, take control.* Sally tried again and reached Claudia to explain the situation.

"So I have a real possibility for a job with the Rockland County Cable Company and you mentioned your lawyer friend and," she had to laugh at the word, "a marker."

"Yes, my girl. That's good news and so soon. FAX it over. I'll have our good buddy check it out. Did the very attractive Lance Jordan treat you well?"

"Yes. I'm in the midst of writing a scenario for the next interview. Meanwhile, I'm finished with the layouts for your ad campaign—Flippin'. There's a lot to choose from. Is Sean in and do you have time today to take a peek?"

"You work fast, Sally. We're busy with clients all afternoon. How about tomorrow morning, say ten o'clock?"

"Time's right for me. See you then."

After sending the contract to Claudia, Sally continued to work on a cohesive sequence for El Mario. Satisfied, knowing Lance would tweak the script, she decided to send it to him with a note about the contract. Keep it simple, stupid—always a good plan and that's how she worded her note. Hit his numbers and pressed send.

A glance at the clock surprised her. Almost time for Steve to return and she didn't have dinner ready. Still wrapped in a damp towel, Sally flew downstairs to the kitchen to select a frozen pork tenderloin for two from the freezer. Placed it on quick defrost, she started risotto rice, Steve's favorite, on to cook in the big saucepan. Like the whirling dervish of long ago, she ran upstairs to change.

When Steve opened the front door, weary after a long day of physical work, he'd sniff the aroma of dinner almost ready. Maybe she'd have time to prepare apple dumplings for dessert.

Chapter 6

Each day brought excitement to the once hum drum life of the homemaker Sally used to be. Today The Silver Belles were gathering for a meet.

Doris's voice called out. "Come on in. The door's open, Sally.

A quick check brought a hidden surveillance camera into Sally's view. She waved, entered a home decorated Southwestern style and stopped to admire large colorful pottery on planked floors with gorgeous Navajo throw rugs. Tan leather couches covered with what looked like handmade cushions tempted her to sit, lie down, take a nap.

"Sally, get in here. Down the hall, make a left."

No hall, Sally thought, just open space and there on the left sat her new friends. "It's not a traditional hall."

"We like wide open spaces so when Monty got a better offer we moved here from Wyoming and built this house to our specifications."

Sally poured hot coffee into a mug. Cinnamon rolls and energy bars were arranged side by side on a handmade pottery plate, a D carved into the design. *Doris made this. What a woman.* "You did yourself proud. Your home is spectacular and I've only seen a small part. Please take me on a tour later."

"Sure." Doris pushed sun-streaked brown hair off her forehead. "Wednesday week we're scheduled for the veteran's hospital. So far we don't have a plan. Ideas?"

"By veteran's, do you mean wounded vets who've returned from combat recently?"

"Yes, Sally. River's Edge is a haven at this point, well staffed with an overflow of wounded recovering men and women who serve our country. We bring in celebrities to visit and perform, do our Silver Belles stuff once a month to give them a laugh. Teresa has a dynamite voice. Teresa, are you well enough to perform next week?"

The slim woman flipped her long gray braid up and down in answer to the question. "The doctor said I'm good to go so I've been vocalizing and selecting some choice music. I've even dusted off the piano keys to accompany me."

"Good girl."

"And you, Sally? Magic tricks, strip tease? You must have hidden talents to share."

Thoughtful for a moment, the new Silver Belle closed her eyes to recall dance, dance and more dance. First a young girl. Then as she grew up. "Bob Fosse."

"What about him?"

"I learned his routines in dance class from a great jazz teacher in Rockland County. Of course this goes way back, but I always do them as a warm-up before exercising. Like from Chorus Line, the big musical on Broadway a long time ago." She jumped up, moved to the planked floor and demonstrated with the exciting jazz steps singing, "One singular sensation ..."

"Wow. Can you teach us this in a week?"

"Uh, no. Don't despair. This will take practice, practice and more practice but you'll love it."

Valerie's husky voice boomed out. "Wait just a second. Why the hell would anyone want to see middle aged women shake their booty's?"

"Trust me, Val. By the time you finish perfecting the moves, you'll be in good shape and we'll wear appropriate costumes according to our age. No thongs and bouncing boobs." Sally rolled her shoulders. "A thought just came to me."

"Like a blinding flash?"

"Yeah, Teresa, just like that. Have you ever had therapy dogs visit the vets?"

Doris shook her head. "I don't know anything about that."

"Well, it just so happens one of my best friends began a program at West Point called Hudson Valley Paws for a Cause. They bring therapy dogs to visit and comfort returning vets and their families. I've seen them at work. I bet when I call Judy, she'll reach out to us and bring trained registered therapy dogs to River's Edge with their owners. In fact, I know just the place to get a van to pick them up. So what do you think?"

"Wait just a darn minute." Valerie paced the big room hands folded behind her back. "Give me an example or five as to how it works. What possible comfort can these trained dogs bring to veterans who've been through a war and return damaged."

"I've seen them in action so I speak with absolute confidence, Val. When the dogs enter a room, right away you feel a sense of blood pressure go down. The dogs are not judgmental about appearance or the sound of a damaged voice so they, with the owner's consent, may go right up to the patient and socialize by nuzzling, always coaxing a smile." Val sat on the floor listening. Teresa and Doris leaned forward. "This brings social interaction, conversing with a friend of the four footed variety. Dogs love to be read to. I've seen a German Shepherd curl up next to a soldier and listen, ears cocked as if he understood every word. And one more thing, dogs love to be brushed. If the veteran is able, hand over a brush and watch love blossom on both sides, human and canine." A big sigh from the Silver Belles affirmed she'd made her point regarding therapy dogs.

Doris, Valerie and Teresa surrounded Sally for a group hug. "I don't know enough about you, new friend, but I'm so glad you moved here."

On that high note, the meeting ended. Sally promised to call Judy Audevard regarding next week's availability and could she round up some therapy dogs and get back to them in the morning. Energy bar in hand, she hurried home.

"Hey Judy, call me..."

"Hey yourself, girlfriend. What's up and I do mean up there in whatchcallit Edgeville."

"River's Edge, the best small town in the northeast so don't make fun." The friends had a good laugh over old times for a few minutes. "You're not busy next Wednesday, are you?"

"You sound serious like it's an 'or else' thingy. Allow me, my demanding pal, to check my calendar."

Sally drummed her fingers on the table, drummed until pink nail polish chipped. Cursed with a mental note to call for a manicure or cure for something.

"All's clear. I don't know how that happened but there it is blank. Maybe a senior moment where I forgot to…"

"No. You're like an elephant who never forgets so fill in the space with River's Edge Veteran's Hospital. Bring Kizzy and two other owners with their therapy dogs. I'll explain in a minute."

"You have some explaining to do right now, you twit! Did you call me an elephant?"

"Did you call me a twit, whatever that might be? Don't take offense. You sound menopausal."

Long silence and sobs. "Yeah. You're right. You're always right and you're not a twit. So explain away."

"I'm in a neighborhood group called the Silver Belles…"

"I love it. Love the name. When can I join?"

"Judy, I'll send you an email with all the information. I suggest, as your BFF, you take a walk, take a nap, engage your sweet husband in some afternoon delight. It always works for me. And for us."

She giggled, hoped Judy listened to her advice and then settled down to work.

Chapter 7

"I've found you at home, Sally." The rich deep tones of Lance Jordan's voice invaded her space. Happy to be alone for a while to work and now he called.

"Hi. I just came in from a neighborhood meeting. There might be an interview worthy project here. I'm mulling it over. You received my ideas for El Mario?" She tingled with anticipation for his answer.

"Let's talk this over at lunch today unless you have another engagement."

Trapped. The next line in a bad movie was your place or mine, big guy. "Oh, fine. Early lunch if that works for you. I have a meeting later this afternoon."

"Nyack. There's a quaint, of course there is an abundance of many quaint shops there, restaurant north on Broadway, off the beaten path. El Sol. 11:45?"

"See you then. I'll bring the approved contract with me and my copy of the sequence of El Mario's interview."

A huff and a puff and Sally ran for the shower to ready herself for lunch with the boss. Gotta wash those pheromones off my skin, she sang as bubbles flew all over the tile walls. Toweling off, she laughed and checked the floor for dead pheromones. Lotion spread on tan skin felt so good. What to wear? She grabbed a pink silk shirt, slim white jeans, a flowered silk scarf and white ankle boots. Once dressed, she approved of her appearance. No time to do anything with her curly hair but run fingers through as she headed down the Palisade Parkway, scuffed leather brief case next to a white summer bag.

Not knowing the location of the restaurant, north of Broadway in Nyack was foreign territory, she used the GPS. Mother's voice greeted her. Startled, Sally almost veered off the road. Steve's mother, a funny, bossy woman deceased a few years ago, agreed to be the voice on their GPS since they couldn't understand the other voices available. *What would Mother think of her driving to meet a handsome man for lunch,* Sally thought. *There would be hell to pay if she knew. Or if Steve found out. Hey, this is business with a thousand dollars for each interview. Big bucks to add to the Atwood coffers. Strictly business. Of course she'd tell Steve about the productive meeting after preparing one of his fave meals and maybe apple pie with a fluted crust.* Damn, too much to think about as she eased into parking next to Lance's car. "Thank you, Mother, for guiding me here." She thought she heard Mother's voice say, "Watch out, daughter-in-law" when she clicked off. *Just my imagination,* she thought and cleared her mind with a shake of her head.

El Sol seemed so familiar. Then Sally remembered the cottage by the Hudson River with the SOLD sign, one of the listings before they drove up to River's Edge. Renovated, enlarged, now it appeared to be a...

"Well, hello Sally. You're right on time."

Hyper excited, Sally backed out of the car dragging her bag and brief case along to hit her leg on the way out. "Hi Lance. I think I've seen this place a while back when it was a cottage. What a pretty view."

White sails on the river billowed with the wind. A race had begun, each sailboat displayed different colors; cheers from the east side echoed across the always cold water. A rainbow of sails crisscrossing in the rush and will to win.

From too close behind her, Lance spoke. "Have you ever sailed?"

"Once long ago, I dated a guy who owned a huge boat. He lived on Long Island Sound and raced. One time he had a party on the boat, a day of sailing. I listened to their sail-speak, tried to find something in common with their women and never saw him again. Not my style."

"What is your style, pretty woman?"

Strictly business, Sally thought, *and pheromones be damned.* "Is brunch served here?"

Cupping her elbow, he led the way into a charming cottage by the Hudson restaurant. She gazed around and realized El Sol was more than an eatery. A discreet notice at the desk offered a Bed and Breakfast arrangement also. What in the world had she gotten into?

212

They were seated outside under an awning with a sweeping view of the river. Sally avoided eye contact with Lance and concentrated on the menu.

"Pancakes. I'd like pancakes and tea. Iced tea."

"And Mr. Jordan, the usual?" The young waiter, shiny black hair cut just so, stood straight.

"No thank you, Arlo. I'll have what my guest ordered. Pancakes are appealing to me right now."

"Lance, obviously you come here often." God, why does every word take on a sexual connotation with him? She couldn't help it. Laughing, she began again. "Lance, you obviously frequent El Sol often."

"You are adorable, Sally. I'm part owner. So of course, I come here often, no pun intended. I saw the property and recognized potential. I called a friend who dabbles in real estate investments. Together we decided it was worth the investment. So far, we're doing well. New kids in town, so to speak. Nice coincidence that you've seen the cottage before and now," he gave a wide gesture with his hands, "here we are."

Arlo brought hot pancakes, syrup and tea for Sally. What she wanted was wine but the drive home required sobriety. A little syrup dripped into the pancakes from a small spout. One taste melted in her hungry mouth. Half way through the meal she glanced up to find Lance watching her, his meal untouched.

"What?" His smoldering gaze heated the syrup as she poured more than enough to drown the half left on her plate. It melted her heart to see the longing in his eyes.

"What, Lance? Are you troubled and need to talk to someone. I'm a good listener and I promise not to tell." She touched his hand about to pat it like a mom does.

"I'm sorry. It's you. Ever since we met I can't get you out of my mind. I'm not sleeping or eating."

"Lance, I'm just a middle aged woman at the beginning of a new phase in my life. I call it spreading my wings. That doesn't mean I'll make the mistake of pushing someone away who has loved me for thirty five years." Fortifying herself with the left-over pancake, she met his sorrowful look, no longer taken in. More confident now, Sally opened the worn case to remove the contract and outline for an interview. "Let's talk business or is this no longer on the table?"

His voice and demeanor changed. After reading the contract, Lance nodded, a satisfied look came over his so handsome face. "Your mine, Sally, in business. I didn't want anyone else to grab your talent before we have a chance to work together." He crossed over to sit next to her, reading the outline for the restaurant interview. "Very good. Better than good. I'll speak to the principals and set a date." So close, once again their eyes met. Lance broke the silence. "Are there any other ideas mulling around in that pretty head?" He pulled a blond curl away from her flushed face.

"Oh yes." With a scrape of the chair, Sally got some space to breathe. She told him about Hudson Valley Paws for a Cause and that they'd be coming to River's Edge the following week, Wednesday, to meet the wounded returning vets at the Veteran's Hospital in River's Edge. "Are you interested in me doing an interview with Judy Audevard and the therapy dogs, with permission of the staff there?"

"Yes. Definitely. I know about the group and the work they do at West Point. Put something together. I'll call the director at the hospital to get an okay for my cable company and you'll be in charge. This is a delicate matter. Your friend, Ms. Audevard, knows her business so follow her lead as to what's appropriate and in good taste."

Relieved brunch ended, Sally rose, bumped into Lance on the way up and found herself wrapped in his powerful arms, their lips together. She didn't break away until his tongue, like a heat seeking missile, plunged into her mouth. She pushed him away with "No." He stopped and steered her out to the car where she'd face the GPS with Mother's disapproving voice giving her directions home. Where she belonged.

"Money makes the world go around, the world go around," she hummed the song from Cabaret once safely away from her new boss who wants to have an affair. No way, no how! Nice dinner for Steve, her loving husband, planned, she stopped for thin sliced chicken on sale, mushrooms, and broccoli. Apples and a pie crust quick mix. Plenty of time to wash that lunch right out of her mind and tongue. Geez!

All of a sudden she thought of Steve's years on the road staying in hotels, conventions, foreign travel, exotic places and several trips to Japan. There must have been many women, lonely nights and Steve, a good looking man on the loose after hours. Men do look around, she'd heard. Even the most faithful. Was he ever unfaithful? There were years of crimes of opportunity possible. And now he's in homes painting with housewives bored and lonely.

She parked in the empty driveway, happy to be home, unhappy at the nasty thoughts that plagued her most of the way to River's Edge. Safe inside, groceries unpacked, Sally ran upstairs to hang her clothes, change into shorts and a tee shirt, brush her teeth and turn some oldies but goodies on the radio. "Don't stop thinking about tomorrow, yesterday's gone, yeah, yesterday's gone." The aroma of good cooking filled the house. She poured a glass of Chardonnay and put her feet up, forgetting to clear the GPS of today's travel.

Chapter 8

The front door opened and slammed shut. For sure, it's not a thief, thought Sally, fresh from another shower. "Steve, are you okay?" She hurried downstairs to greet her usually affable husband.

He grumped into the kitchen , the sound of work boots clunked against the beautiful front door, a scowl on his sweaty face. After opening the skillet filled with simmering chicken and mushrooms in wine sauce, he peered into the oven to see one of his favorite apple pies with the fluted crust Sally made so well.

At last he looked up to find his wife who waited for an answer to her question.

"So you drove all the way down to Nyack to a place called El Sol for what or is it too personal to ask?"

She thought fast with nothing too much too hide with the exception of a hot kiss from Lance. That damn GPS. Steve had always checked mileage and gas when he was in corporate business for expense purposes. The habit stayed with him so when in doubt, he asked Mother, the GPS voice, who never lied.

"I have great news. I signed a six month contract with Rockland Cable Corporation. One thousand dollars per interview. One is already in the can and two more are good possibilities."

"And that required a trip to Nyack?"

"Well, yes. I had to meet the boss somewhere and the closest was north Nyack."

Brushing past her husband, she turned the oven off and carefully removed the pie. The crust had a touch of toasty brown; cinnamon apples bubbled inside. She turned the burner on the range to off. The click had an ominous sound to it. Deep inside Sally simmered from the interrogation instead of having a pleasant conversation at day's end. Dinner ready, she set the table.

"If you're as hungry as I am, wash your hands and let's sit." Without waiting for an answer, Sally opened a chilled bottle of Pinot Grigio to pour into wine glasses.

Sally could not remember them ever having such a dinner, the stony silence oppressive. Like a defendant waiting for the verdict after a long trial, she sat, all taste gone from the meal prepared with loving care. Finally she tasted a forkful l of the main course and sighed. He would get over his misplaced anger and she'd enjoy this meal.

"Mmm. Delicious, if I must say so myself. As I recall, this is one of your favorite meals." She laughed. "You've always had a good appetite though and I'm thrilled you're taking an interest in cooking."

Her grumpy husband ladled more food onto his plate and kind of grunted like a caveman. Stifling the urge to bop him over the head with the serving spoon, Sally added more mushrooms and sauce to her plate to cover the chicken. The silence hung heavy despite every effort of Sally's to brighten the dinner. One more try.

"Steve, this is very good news for us. The contract assures us of extra income for at least six months. We'll keep a strict budget and save our money. Maybe we can take a vacation, enjoy our time alone."

He wiped his mouth, the frown remained on his face.

"What troubles me is this, Sally. In all of our years together, I've been the breadwinner, the provider for you and the kids. Now I'm reduced to being a kind of broken down handyman after the company downsized and threw me under the bus. And you have blossomed into a hot looking wage earner." He held up a calloused hand to stop her from speaking. "More than that, you're a person who will be known for her creativity married to a guy who paints houses." That said, Steve cleared the dinner dishes and set the apple pie between them. Cutting two slices, he placed them on dainty dessert plates, his once smooth hands carefully set one for her and one larger slice for him .

After tasting the first bite, he smiled. "Hmm. Delicious, Sally. You always made the best pies." He scraped the plate clean and licked the fork. "Remember the bake sales for the PTA?" She nodded, happy to see him recover from the spill of hurt. "Your pies were the first to go." He leaned forward to take her hand. "I had so much pride in what you accomplished in the kitchen. And now I'm afraid of losing you to a world I'm not familiar with. It scares me, Sally. Really scares me."

She climbed on his lap like a kid but he needed comfort and she held her big bear of a husband tight.

"I had no idea you worried about—what's the word?"

"Status, so popular on Facebook. In our day family lines were clear. Me Tarzan—you Jane." He chuckled.

"So true. But honey, I don't work 9 to 5 at an office. It's creative work at home like an author or an artist. And the pay is great to benefit both of us. Maybe because Lance Jordan is wealthy, he's giving me a big chunk of money because I'm a find. Someone new he can boast about if I'm successful. If not, six months goes by fast and I'll be out on my butt searching for something else. But I don't think so, Steve. I have a good feeling about this job."

There were tears in Steve's eyes. "I'm afraid of being left behind, Sally."

"Not possible, sweetheart. This is a bump in the long road we've traveled together. I depend on your approval of the interviews. You were spot on regarding the first one with Grace Trumbull. You've had years of business experience to know what sounds and looks right in presentations. "

They kissed, the taste of cinnamon lingered on their tongues.

Full dark crept over the house at the end of the winding road shielding the troubled couple as they reached for each other on the late summer night. With no intrusion to disturb them, Sally and Steve found beauty in the pleasure of their bodies. She removed her tee shirt. With the familiarity of years, Steve dabbed apple juices from the pie on her bare nipples and sucked them dry.

"An aperitif better than any other."

She did the same to him. In a tangle of dropped clothes, they hurried upstairs to continue the joy they found in each other.

After the loving, Steve fell asleep. Snuggled close to her husband, Sally's thoughts turned to another. *Beware of him. Your best interests are not his. He wants much more from his new reporter.* Satisfied with sex and a new found worldly education, she slept.

"We'll be fine, sweetheart." Steve kissed his precious wife before leaving to finish the job where the woman of the house lingered far too long while he worked, offered way too many refreshments and swayed her curvy ass in a provocative way. How easy it would be to compromise a good marriage and just the thought of another man taking Sally for lunch enraged him. Adjustments were in order for both of them.

He called from the car. "How about salmon with your special Hollandaise sauce over asparagus tonight? I know you're busy but if it's not too much trouble? Am I whining?"
Sally giggled. "Never too much trouble for you, dear."

Smiling, she dressed fast to hurry over to the local Buy Everything Super Market in town before the store got crowded. She'd left a call to Judy who was long gone at a senior facility with Hudson Valley Paws for a Cause. She needed a clear picture of what goes on from the time the dogs and owners arrived at the Veteran's Hospital from beginning to the end of the visit. How long do they stay and the whole program. It was a lot to ask of Judy and her friends. In all the years she and Judy had been friends, they'd never let each other down.
The weather changed. Sally felt it in her bones. Summer heat turned just a bit cooler; leaves once bright green now bore a tinge of gold and orange hue.
Annie, the chief of the sea food counter, greeted her with a big grin. "So early, Ms. Atwood. What can I do you for?"
"Hi Annie. The big guy needs his fix of salmon fillet with the skin off the back just the way only you do can do it. One pound, please." Annie disappeared behind cold doors and Sally's eye's roamed around the relatively empty store.
She spied a young man, cute with a good haircut, no grocery cart to push. Curious, she moved closer after Annie handed over the package. Always the observer, Sally noticed him talking to a male employee in a hushed tone. The young guy made straight for the pharmacy department. Sally pushed her cart close feigning interest in sunglasses right next to the condoms. A big display of those wonder male needs. Women, too. Now they came in different colors and

textures from what Steve told her. In their day, one size fit all, maybe. The cute guy read several packages , decided on two big assortments and concealing them in his hand and kind of up his sleeve, with a sly smile on his handsome face he strode fast to the fresh flower department conveniently located across from the pharmacy. Marketing 101. After selecting a bouquet of yellow roses wrapped with a big bow, he paid for his purchases and ran out of the store.

All in the hopes of getting laid. *Good luck, young man. You have no idea how much fun you've provided for the newbie reporter this morning.*

After buying the few items on her list, Sally headed home. She wondered how to use this amusing non-encounter to her advantage. No interview material here but maybe an article for Cosmo or one of the many magazines in the marketplace. She knew how to write funny. Over dinner tonight, she'd discuss this with Steve, her best pal. Add a little spice to more than the salmon.

Chapter 9

Happy to be home, Sally found an email from Judy with a terrific detailed description of the chain of events to take place at the Veteran's Hospital. Obviously Judy used the trick Sally taught her years ago called Picture This. You picture a scene in your mind allowing all of your emotions to enter and then write. And Judy did just that. *Good enough*, she thought. Better than good; enough to spark her own creative juices to flow. Sally wrote a complete scenario to FAX to Lance. *No more opportunities for seduction, my handsome boss. Strictly business.* She pushed Send.

The next call went to Doris, head of the Silver Belles. "Hi Doris, I have four therapy dogs committed for next week. We need permission from the chief administrator at the hospital."

"No problem, Sally. Thanks for putting the program together. It seems Lance Jordan contacted his old friend who agreed to discreet filming of an interview." Doris's husky voice dropped to a confidential tone. "How did you pull it off, you with your curly blond hair and unassuming manner. There's more to you than meets the eye."

Heat rushed to Sally's cheeks. No confiding in anyone. She needed a dog with a sympathetic ear. A no-tell friend. The sad saluki came to mind but no. He needed his own pal. She'd go to the Pet Emporium and ask Grace.

"Doris, I ask and sometimes I get an affirmative answer. That's all. Talk to you later."

OPEN, the sign proclaimed outside the Pet Emporium. Inside, the sound of meowing greeted Sally. She never had a cat. You didn't have to walk them in the rain or snow. Just a litter box , feed them and what else? She didn't have a clue.

A woman with a long dark brown braid said, "Hi. I'm Petra. This is Queen. She's a year old Persian purebred someone left at the door this morning. Why anyone would abandon such an amazing feline is cruel and sad. Fortunately Queen is in the right place."

Sally reached out to touch the gorgeous cat with sparkling jade green eyes. She stroked behind her pointed ears and under her small chin. To Sally's surprise, loud meowing came from the cat as if she wanted to chat. "Oh my. I thought she'd make a little purr in her throat."

"Persians are great companions. They follow you around the house chatting away, hanging out. I just might take her home unless, of course, you're interested. Think it over. Are you here to see Grace and Scott? They're out back, having a moment with the kids." Petra pointed to a door. "There." She walked away with Queen who seemed to call to Sally.

Her heart ached for the abandoned cat. Wondering what circumstances led the owner to just leave, walk away. Illness, a calamity of epic proportions? She'd have to discuss it with Steve, wouldn't she? With one more longing gaze at the beautiful feline carried by Petra, she headed for the door.

And then she entered a wonderland of flowers. Trees, a dog run, bird feeders everywhere and a playground of large proportions with swings and climbing steps, ladders and a playhouse. A wicker lounge chair for two where basking in the sun, hands entwined, were Scott and Grace.

"Oh, I'm interrupting your private time. Petra said to open the door."

Twins narrowly missed bumping into Sally as they raced around in circles on tricycles. Grandchildren, she noted from the resemblance to both Grace and Scott. A boy and a girl. "How adorable. This scene takes me way back when our kids were little. Now our youngest son John and his bride are expecting in a few months."

"Sally, what a pleasant surprise. Meet our grandkids, Lily and Lenny."

The close to three year old twins danced around Sally. "Granny carried us in her tummy." They ran to their tricycles and rode around her in circles.

Scott's wife's infectious laugh set the twins to giggling. "Shall we reveal our not so secret, Gracie? Since the beans were spilled the minute Sally walked in..."

Grace shrugged. "Those little blabber mouths. We adore them but sometimes we need a gag order for two.

Okay, if you have time and you're interested, Scott and I have an interesting background. This is not an interview, Sally. It's just a confidential conversation between friends."

Forgetting family problems, Sally pulled a lounge chair closer.

'I'm definitely interested and I don't want to miss a word."

Grace began in her enthusiastic way. "We met in college, a few months before graduation. The year was 1960. Scott was the big man on campus and I, well, I was the studious girl at nineteen and way younger in every way than the other girls on campus."

Scott interjected, "Nineteen and never been kissed. Grace intrigued me, so studious, concentrating on books, never dating. She didn't live on campus."

Grace blushed. "He said we should go to the beach."

"You said that, Gracie."

For just a moment Sally was aware Grace had tuned in to another time.

"Yes, I'm the culprit. When Scott kissed me, my very first kiss, I was knocked for a loop. He had all that experience and..."

Excited, Scott recalled, "We had burgers on the way back to campus and she pointed to a building where she lived and I almost fell over when she asked me to come up."

"It was the beginning of an affair, short lived when I discovered I was pregnant all because I didn't say no."

"As much my fault as yours, sweetheart."

"Afraid to tell Scott and ruin his plans for his future, I ran away. My, uh, parents would have nothing to do with me. Fortunately my grandfather left me major bucks so I turned around and with the kindness of strangers I found my way to River's Edge. I met Jim Trumbull, my first husband, who opened the Pet Emporium with me and raised our daughter until he passed on. By our, I mean mine and Scott's."

Sally wiped tears on a napkin and drank the ever present sweet tea while in the background, the twins were playing in a huge sand box. "What happened next?"

"Scott, feel free to jump in any time."

"I searched for Grace but couldn't find her. I even went way up north to her parents who wouldn't open the door so I enrolled in the Police Academy at John Jay College in New York, studied hard, made a disastrous marriage ending even worse than it began and then joined the K 9 Unit and met my dog, King. And here's where the story becomes fun. A few years ago, I took a day off and drove with my trusty pal, King to a wonderful park not far from here. It was getting late and with no one around, I removed King's lead so he could run the way they do at a dog park. Bad idea turned to change our lives, right, Gracie?"

Again her delightful laugh rang out across the big back yard. "Oh yes."

"King had a too close encounter with a skunk and there we were in the dark where I didn't know anyone. I did recall seeing the Pet Emporium sign on Main Street so driving just fast enough and smelling way terrible, I opened the door and yelled Skunk. This beauty called hurry up and together we poured like eight cans of tomato juice over King and me until finally we were clean and then we looked at each other. The shock of recognition! She invited us upstairs to the apartment above the shop. We talked for hours catching up."

"Lasagna. Don't forget I ordered lasagna. And we looked through albums of pictures of our daughter from infancy to marriage and finally I told him I was pregnant with our daughter's baby. Surrogate since she had so much trouble carrying to term. "

"That's close to the whole story, Sally. Just about everyone in town knows part of it and now you know most of how we came to be together."

Sally kissed both of them. "Thanks for the best story I've ever heard." She looked toward the twins throwing sand at each other. "You carried those babies for your daughter just a few years ago. You're one helluva mom. I don't know if I'd ever do that for my girls."

"You stopped by to see us for what? Just a friendly visit? You certainly got more than you expected, I'm sure." Scott poured more tea and waited.

"Frankly I need a no-tell companion like a dog or maybe that Persian cat abandoned today. What a beauty. I don't have a girlfriend here, a confidante I can trust. Doris from my neighborhood started asking personal questions on the phone. I realized I wasn't going to tell her anything she would repeat so I gave her an oblique answer and hung up. Then I came here. "

Grace reached for Scott's hand. "What about your husband? Can you confide in him?"

"Sure, about most things but sometimes there's stuff I can't tell Steve because he'll get upset. I've always been a homemaker and he's been the breadwinner. Our lives have changed in a big way since moving here. We have adjustments to make. So what do you think about a dog or cat?"

The wind picked up causing sand to blow in Lily's eyes. She cried and ran to Scott who scooped her up in his strong loving arms. Lenny followed, also crying to show a boo boo to Grace and Sally. They made a big fuss over the delicious kids.

"Let's go in. I suggest you take Queen home for a test ride. Persians are talkative and fun. Good companions and they love to play ball. If you want a dog, they get along well with canines. Let Steve see if Queen suits your household. We'll give you the carry case she came in plus kibbles and a box with litter and some cat food. If you love her, keep her. Then we'll see about a mellow pooch to walk and have more fun with after a hard day's work."

Again Grace thanked them, hugged the little ones and helped Scott pack the car with the cat and her belongings. On the way home, Queen kept her company. Sally spoke her thoughts out loud and her new pal seemed to listen and advise. When she said, "Do you think Steve will like you?" she could have sworn, Queen meowed loud and clear, "You betcha."

Chapter 10

By the time Sally arrived home with a roasted chicken ready for dinner purchased at the store, Queen making a racket in the backseat ready to come out, she needed to race back and forth unloading food, cat and all supplies to be ready for Steve's homecoming. Warmed by the charming story of Grace and Scott, she scurried around, first to set up the litter box on the basement landing. Next came Queen who meowed something like, "It's about time," when Sally opened the cat carrier. Elegant, her green eyes taking in her new home, she sauntered out, pausing to sniff this corner and that to find the box. And find it she did.

When Sally opened a can of salmon cat food, she showed up even before half the contents emptied in a small tin. Daintily she licked her platter clean. Next came a cleaning ritual of paws, face and lean body. Afterward, Queen curled up in a cat bed and napped. Transfixed, the new cat owner watched to snap out of her trance when the sound of a truck warned of Steve's arrival.

Fast, she washed her hands, got a salad together, peeled an avocado, opened a can of black olives, sliced thin red onions and opened the container of chicken. Boots thumped near the door as it opened. Steve sniffed dinner's aromas.

"Hi honey, I'm home."

Yay! A lilt to his voice brought happiness to her heart. *Please let him like Queen.* "I got home a little while ago. I was at the Pet Emporium. They told me the most charming story of how they met and re-met and..."

"And who is this?" Steve cradled Queen in his arms. They looked eye to eye, her purring loud and so sweet.

"Her name is Queen. She's a Persian someone abandoned this morning. Scott and Grace gave her to us with your approval, of course. They also added cat food, a bed, litter box and a toy. She likes to play ball and loves dogs. Purebred as you can see and only a year old in excellent health."

So much for the build-up. She waited for his response. He sniffed her. She sniffed him. He stroked her back, under her neck and around her pointed ears. She licked his hand and talked to him.

"I think I'm in love, Sally. Where's the ball?"

Sally found the red cotton ball with green feathers and rolled it to him. Queen did a flying leap and raced to get it. She grabbed it with sharp teeth and ran back to Steve to drop it at his feet. "This is a ball?" Steve laughed and threw the toy. Before it landed, Queen leapt high to catch it.

When Sally said, "Dinner's ready," he groaned, "Already? We're having so much fun."

The extra special salad with layers of Romaine, sliced chicken, avocado, slivers of red tomatoes, cold black olives , a sprinkle of red onion slice thin topped by grated cheese set up pretty in crystal bowls. They sat. Suddenly pointy brown ears appeared at the third chair. The gorgeous green eyes and elegant head of Queen surveyed the table. The proud beauty came to dinner.

The Atwood's didn't know whether to laugh or scold. Policy making time.

"Should we let her stay?"

"I'm too hungry right now to make a decision. Delicious salad, honey. You know it's another one of my favorites."

"After thirty-five years, I know. Believe me, I know what you like."

Queen purred, joining the dinner conversation. "One rule we must establish. No table scraps for Queen. She eats cat food and kibbles."

"Right." Steve mashed a piece of chicken up so fine and with his fingers, scooped it up to put right in front of their new pet.

Queen tilted her head one way and then the other, stretched her long neck to sniff this gift and her tongue did the rest. Plate clean.

"Steve, we just agreed not to feed her from the table."

"Not. I said right but she's so sweet and polite and doesn't beg, I had to give her a taste of your fine chicken."

"You'll be punished for insubordination, young man."

"I hope so." And the happy couple finished dinner.

After dinner, they went out to the screened-in porch; Queen scooted right after them to sit on the swing for two, now three.

"About the cat, she's never to go outside. It's not safe so make sure she doesn't run after you when you open the doors."

"Okay. We could put her on a leash."

"No. Cats don't like that and there are all kinds of germs in the grass to make her sick."

They rocked on the old swing, lulled by the magic of a late summer night. Cicadas sang, an owl hooted in response and fireflies, like tiny flash lights, lit up the fenced yard. Queen added to the cacophony of the night with contented loud purrs.

"It doesn't get much better than this, does it?" Steve caressed Sally's cheeks which led to more loving touches and soon, the second honeymoon continued. Queen had the good sense to curl up in a chair and take a nap.

When they crawled into bed later, Steve made an offhand comment. "So where does Queen sleep?" Loud purring answered him.

Sally rushed downstairs to return with a cozy pink cat bed. She held their new pet in her arms, stroked her shorthair coat and soon the twin green pools of Queen's eyes closed. Just like a baby, Sally gently laid her down.

Spooned with her own warm hunk, he'd become muscular with fat burned off from physical work, they slept to awake too early in the morning to the sound of paper ripping nearby. One eye open, Steve saw his favorite newspaper torn to shreds with a happy cat running around, shredded news hanging from her mouth.

"Cat-astrophe!" he said.

Sally cracked up to think at last his sense of humor had returned.

"I know just what to do."

"What?"

"There's a pet supply store on Main Street. I can run over and get one of those scratch and climbing gizmos I've seen in a couple of the houses I've painted. Queen can scratch and do whatever cats do and leave my newspaper the hell alone."

"Good idea, honey. While you're up, please empty the litter box. Bags are in the kitchen closet."

As long as they were up, Sally put the coffee on and scrambled eggs, fed the cat and got a wash going. After breakfast Steve drove off in the white truck with the new logo Sally designed. Zipitty-do-da-day; FLIP your House the Trumbull Realtor way. The phone number painted underneath. Claudia had called to say the response was great. Already they had more customers than they expected.

He returned a half an hour later beaming. "Help me carry this in."

After setting up two cat condominiums, they laughed in amazement as their genius feline flew through the air landing at the top of the tallest one and promptly dozed off.

"Sally, I love River's Edge. Where else could I have bartered for all of this cat stuff by suggesting I paint their shop. Jimmy Clements, the owner, threw in some toys for our new baby. It's like an old fashioned town where neighbors look after each other."

Chapter 11

This was Sally's first experience at a Veteran's Hospital. She knew from talking to Judy how she and her friends felt. Nervous, heart beating fast and now it was her turn to look down a corridor at a sea of soldiers, some with missing arms and legs; some with bandaged faces and heads. But it was the eyes. Oh, dear God, their eyes that gripped Sally's heart. She heard the sound of muffled conversation, not much laughing. Soldiers with I Pads or watching movies in the TV alcove.

And then someone wonderful took her by the arm. "Ms. Atwood, I'm Celine Lawrence. Thank you for bringing Hudson Valley Paws for a Cause here. They've done wonders at West Point and now it's our turn. Lance Jordan called and cleared the way. We discussed the protocol regarding a digital recording of the interview. I'll be the final judge before we allow it on cable television.

"Dr. Lawrence, I'm so happy to meet you. I'm the new member of the Silver Belles. New at most everything, since we moved to River's Edge not long ago."

"Call me Celine, please. The kids call me Doc." She gestured to the many veterans. The Belles are so much fun when they come here. I can't wait 'til their next visit and we have you to thank for the therapy dogs coming today."

Sally gulped, stunned by her poise, titian red hair held back in an amber clip and eyes so like Queen, her new cat, sparkling emerald green that didn't miss anything even as they spoke. She immediately made a plan to transfer Lance's affection for her to this beautiful doctor. No ring on her finger but that didn't mean much.

"Celine, this may be too intimate a question to ask but are you married?"

"No, are you?" A touch of humor accompanied the good doctor's answer.

"Yes, thirty-five years. Thanks. It's my curious reporter's mind snooping. Moving on," Sally checked her watch, "The bus with Judy Audevard and her friends, Pat and Susan and their therapy dogs should be pulling up just about now. Along with the techies, I'm proud to say. Lance Jordan, the boss will oversee the shoot to insure we do it right."

"I've had the pleasure of meeting the gentleman."

"You're referring to Lance?"

Her smile had a touch Mona Lisa when she said his name. "Just the other day he came to check out our hospital, he said. Make sure he brought enough light and technicians, he said. He said a lot of things including an invitation to lunch. We dined at our fine ," Celine arched an eyebrow, "cafeteria with the techies, a terrific group of experienced people. Smooth talker, don't you agree?"

Sally stifled a desire to laugh out loud. Instead she grinned. "Yes, smooth is the word. I see everything is set for the shoot. I guess the folks are hanging out waiting to begin. Is Lance here somewhere? He's always on time, early in fact."

"I was too busy in the office so I have no idea."

"Do I hear the roar of a truck?"

"And barking dogs. Greet the group and after the dogs do their business outside, they're welcome , so very welcome to be our guests. Thanks, Sally. I'm excited and so are the men and women here."

Sally hurried outside to find Judy and Kizzy, a white curly haired Bichon Frise, just climbing out of the comfortable truck hired for the trip to River's Edge. Judy's friends, Susan , tall and slender who even after the trip, was perky. The veterans would love her. She brought two dogs, one a yellow Lab named Darla and her younger brother Douglas, the black Lab known for exuberant greetings who loves to be petted at your feet. What's not to be crazy about these special canines. Sally turned to see Pat with blond hair and a peaches and cream complexion you could die for. Pat had her German Shepherd, Jessie, on a leash.

"I can't thank you enough for coming up here."

The three women wore red tee shirts with Hudson Valley Paws for a Cause logo. You couldn't miss them anywhere. Sally had a sense of pride well up just looking at them.

Judy hugged her old pal. "So where's the money?" The friends were always finding ways to make each other laugh.

Cameras ready for action, we walked down the hall and as if on cue, the dogs went to work.

They didn't see the heartbreak of damaged people. They saw people. People who would give them treats, pets and hugs.

"The dogs are here!" was like a war cry of joy. Soldiers hobbled on crutches, wheeled themselves in chairs and came closer to the dogs and their owners. A circle formed and grew until everyone who was able joined in to catch a good look at the special dogs. Sally moved away to became part of the background with the sea of veterans who were now a circle of friends.

Tails wagging, the trained therapy canines greeted each member of the circle. Eyes shining, some soldiers whistled for attention. Some started talking about their own pets back home. One pretty vet, arm and one leg wrapped up, spoke of the pup she'd raised and how much she missed her. Once muffled sounds became excited chatter unleashing feelings held in check too long. Darla, the yellow Lab barked hello and waved a paw causing more laughter. Her little brother, the black Lab, bounded down to greet the veterans with great enthusiasm until he fell to the floor and waited for petting and treats. Then Jessie, the big German Shepherd played a peek-a-boo game and carried a basket of toys around with balls to play fetch and brushes for any soldier who wanted to brush a dog's coat while the big canine snuggled up.

Sally checked with the techies who were placed in strategic positions so as not to miss a moment. She noticed wet sleeves on Gino from wiping tears. She knew how he felt. It took all her will power to hold back sniffles. "Thumbs up, everyone?" The response was positive. They'd never forget today and how lucky they were. Lucky and grateful to these young men and women warriors who protected our country. Lance hung back. Sally had a feeling he'd be proud to have the ability to bring this to public attention.

And Kizzy, Sally loved Judy's pup, decided to take center stage. Funny and adorable, as soon as he sensed an audience, he went into his tricks routine. He did high fives, danced, rolled over and stood like a statue. A born clown with a loving heart, he extracted treats from his audience in payment and allowed scratches behind the ears.

The dogs bowed for everyone when it was time to leave. Applause and cheers from a grateful audience.

All Sally thought was God Bless them all, these wounded veterans, for what they've done for us. She made it to the door to thank Judy, Pat and Susan for their time and energy today. "Judy, before I forget, "she handed her friend a blue jar, "here's the cream for your poor knee. Happy bending."

"Thanks, Pal Doc."

"Wait just a sec." Pat and Susan hurried to grab Sally's arm. "We need an appointment to your uh, Pal Doc free clinic."

"Judy's got my number. Anytime, Ladies." Flushed with grateful relief that the afternoon went so well, Sally had one more thing to say. "Now for a real treat. There's a gourmet dinner for all of you at The River's Edge 5 Star Restaurant down the road. A good friend, the owner Larry Owen, invites you and your four footed companions to come right now. You won't regret it."

"Our dogs, too?"

"Larry's a dog lover as you'll see."

Kisses, hugs and the truck roared off down the road. *Hold your tears, Sally. Watch the video and go home. Cry later.*

Chapter 12

The cable team gathered equipment. Sally walked around. "What do you think? Did you catch a lot of good moments?"

Maryanne gazed at her with red eyes. "We have enough for a series. I mean it."

Charlie , the leader, shook his longish blond hair. "Don't worry. We'll look closely at every frame and consolidate. Maybe get it down to thirty minutes. Really. It's so worth the watching. "

"Listen up, people." Sally had an inspiration. We'll order pizzas. Eat at my house close by and do a preliminary check to see what we have."

The response was immediate. "Way cool. I'm hungry. Let's go." And Lance walked in. "What's this all about?"

"Pizza, boss. At Sally's house. Like now... and we'll review what we have. And then the gang will go home and see you tomorrow unless you want to stay for pizza done up the River's Edge way." Sally had a sense of pride that the gang listened to her, the newbie reporter making plans.

Lance took a deep breath and looked at his employees. "You all did a remarkable job here today, inconspicuous in your focus to capture the essence of the scene. Wounded vets responding to therapy dogs. It will touch the public's heart. It touched mine and you know it takes a lot to do that." Laughter from the kids. "So thanks. And to Sally, I'm indebted to you for putting this together. You have brought some creative dynamics to our cable company."

Before she knew it, the handsome boss pulled her into his arms for a big kiss.

"As for me, I'm having dinner with Doctor Lawrence tonight. See you all tomorrow. Early. We have a lot to do."

"Wow." Gino gaped. "Boss never kissed me like that."

"I hope not. It's reserved for beautiful women." Charlie slung an equipment bag over his shoulder. "Let's go. It's been a long afternoon."

Lance Jordan's swan song in front of the crew, Sally thought. Odd and now he moved on. She hoped he'd find the right woman this time.

Steve returned home to find a party in full swing with Fleetwood Mac on DVD, three strangers gathered, slice in one hand, beer in the other and Sally grinning.

"Hey gang, meet my hubby, the best guy ever. Steve meet the kids, the techies superb, Charlie, Maryanne, and Gino. We're celebrating a great important shoot so pick up a slice of your fave and join the party. We're just about ready to check out footage from the Veteran's Hospital." Her voice changed when she spoke the last two words, all gaiety drained from her.

Steve waved, his calloused hand grimy. "Hi all. I'll be ready in a minute."

Boots dropped on the mat at the door, he hurried to wash his hands. Queen purred a greeting from the highest perch. Steve stopped to give a scratch behind her ears. Preening, she accepted his affection.

The living room took on a hushed atmosphere when Steve returned. Charlie set up a screen. The story unfolded. The five of them leaned forward to watch and listen. The dogs enter the long corridor. As soon as they're seen, the veteran's form a ragged circle of wheelchairs, patients on crutches. Laughs, cheers.

Charlie said, "Cut One, agreed?"

Maryanne sniffled. "Yeah. Great beginning."

"Widen to see more faces. Just sayin'." Gino shrugged.

"Gino, I disagree. Get an overall visual and slow scan the expressions."

Steve didn't say a word. He munched on a slice and drank beer watching, eyes glued to the screen.

When it ended, the now silent crew gathered their equipment.

"Remarkable work." Steve shook hands with each of them. "I'm certain the finished product will be..." Steve stopped. "Thanks all of you."

Charlie gripped his hand tight. "Sally's told us about your long background in business, experience with presentations and interviews. We could use a person like you on our team."

"Whoa. Technologically speaking, I'm left way behind. I'm honored you think I'd be helpful so if you ever need me to have a look and offer my humble opinion, give a shout out."

Charlie grinned. "Okay then. Thanks for your hospitality and pizza. See you, Sally, early tomorrow. We have our work cut out for us. 'Night."

The minute the door clicked shut, Steve picked up his wife in newly developed muscular arms and twirled her around.

"You're a constant wonder to me, Sally." Breathless, he set her down. "When we met , we were kids. You learned to be a terrific wife and mother. And now you're this talented creative woman." He kissed her with such tenderness, she wanted to cry.

"Time for bed, honey. We both have a full day tomorrow. Don't forget, Claudia and Larry expect us for dinner at his house at eight."

"Tomorrow night?"

"Yes. I had to cancel once so we're on. I'll pick up a little something for them on the way home."

"Can we bring Queen?"

She threw a pillow at him. "Time for bed."

Chapter 13

What do you bring as a gift to a couple, not married, when you're invited to dinner? Sally pondered the impossible. He's the owner of a 5 star restaurant and she's been incredibly generous to us, newcomers in this town we've come to love. Hmm. All the way back from Rockland Cable Company, she thought and thought. How about something for his dog? He never goes anywhere without the gorgeous Lab. She parked in front of the Pet Supply shop. *They really need a different name*, Sally thought.

"Hi, Kerry. I so need your help. For the dog who has everything. Any suggestions?"

Kerry laughed. "You must be talking about Larry Owen's yellow Lab Sam."

"I am."

"Well," her forehead wrinkled, "How about a winter coat? Larry walks him every day no matter the weather and it sure does get cold up here."

"A dog coat?"

"Just a sec." Kerry hurried to the back of the shop. Sally browsed for something for Queen. After a few minutes, Kerry returned with a Sherpa coat fit for a King. "This coat was new on the market last year. We have one left in Sam's size XL and I'll give it to you half price." When Sally shook her head no, Kerry said, "Steve's going to renovate our shop. He has terrific ideas so don't you dare turn away our good will, young lady."

"Thanks so much. Gift wrap please with a nice big bow." She paid the bill and hurried home.

The Atwoods had never been to this part of town. Set back in a private old community, a lifestyle existed they'd never seen before. Like the Hollywood movies from years gone by, homes sheltered by huge trees and sculpted bushes were protected from view. They searched for and found Larry's home tucked way back behind an iron fence, a voice called. "Your name, please."

Sally giggled. "Steve and Sally Atwood are visiting guests this evening." Steve lowered his voice to impress the inquisitor. The gate slid open. They drove in, their shining BMW freshly washed for the special occasion. Through many curves and finally round a bend, they arrived at an imposing home with a portico of tall columns and immaculate flower beds trimmed to perfection.

Sally whispered, "Big house for a single man and one dog. Must be an old family estate." Steve nodded and escorted his wife out into the fragrant lavender scented summer air. He carried the gift.

"Good evening." A man of medium height dressed meticulously in a dark suit and a silk tie with an artist's drawing of Sam painted on the front greeted them. "I am Roger and you are the Atwood's. Larry and Claudia are in the drawing room eager to see you. Follow me."

He led them down a wide hall past several carved wood doors to what he called the drawing room. "Tada! Your guests are here and right on time." The Grandfather clock struck eight.

Sam bounded off one of many couches, first to say or bark hello. He sniffed the package Steve held.

"Sam, sit." He obeyed his master's voice.

Arms opened wide, both Claudia and Larry rose to say hello.

After hugs, Sally gave the gift to Larry. "For Sam. I hope he likes it and that it fits."

Claudia ripped open the package and exclaimed. "Just what Sam needs. A Sherpa coat for winter. Thank you both and XL is his size."

"Sit over here. That's Sam's couch, spoiled canine. What's your pleasure?"

Larry offered a choice of wine before dinner with an assortment of cheese on a tray on the marble table.

"I'll have Pinot Grigio and Sally, usually you like Chardonnay. Right?"

"So right. Thanks. We've never driven up this way before. A very old established community tucked away from everything. It's beautiful. Larry, did you grow up here?"

"Bingo. You hit it. My parents built this house expecting to fill it with many children. Alas I'm an only child who grew up with dogs, guns, love of fine food and how it's prepared due to the expert chef who lived here. Thus the restaurant and Roger, my eccentric friend who came, stayed and conquered all of us. The chef was his father, gone long ago to the kitchen in the sky, leaving Roger in charge of me and all the household staff."

He pulled Claudia into his arms. "Before we venture into marriage at our age, we've invited you for dinner for a dual purpose. First because we like you and second, we need advice."

"Counseling before we take the huge step." Claudia interjected.

Dumbfounded, the Atwoods stared at them. "What could we possibly suggest to help you? You're both established, successful people already." Sally took a big swig of wine and almost choked.

"Yes to all that, but Sally, we've never been married and don't know about the how to do it like you do. After thirty five years together, you know the secret." Claudia's blue eyes streamed with tears.

Oh. The secret. Let me count the ways, Sally thought. Her eyes sparkled gazing at Steve. "Pen and paper, please." Roger on the spot handed them to her and disappeared again. "Steve, together we'll make the list." He gave her a thumbs up.

Always remember Marriage is one long conversation. Communication keeps you out of trouble!

The grass is NEVER greener on the other side so be faithful or it's curtains for both of you.

She nibbled on some extraordinary Jarlsberg cheese as she thought.

Never go to bed angry.

Kiss goodnight and good morning.

Love your one and only and love good. Don't be shy. Try new ways to please each other.

She looked up to find their friends nodding.

"Steve, you must have something to add."

"Yeah, I definitely do. For a while, I started looking in my rear view window and one day, not long ago, I realized that I was looking at the past and missing what lies ahead. My future is here alone with Sally in this wonderful town. So what if I lost my job. That's gone. So long, good bye. I began again forward step by step doing the best I can with Sally by my side."

Somewhere in the big house, a dinner bell rang. They all stood and walked toward the future.

The Beginning...Not The End

More Great Books by Charmaine Gordon

ALSO IN AUDIOBOOK! OPTIONED FOR TELEVISION MOVIE!

To Be Continued

Elizabeth Malone wakes up the morning after an amazing night of passion with her husband of forty years to find a note: Dear Lizzie, it's not you, it's me. Abandoned by her husband, disappointed in daughter Susie's casual attitude Dad's having a mid-life crisis, Beth decides to re-establish herself as the winner she once was. When Frank Malone returns, he's in for a big surprise!

Starting Over

Each morning, Emily Kendrick runs on the hard-packed sand of St. Augustine Beach to clear her mind and heal her heart. From the widow's walk of the house perched high on the dunes, a man trains his binoculars on Emily…

Now What?

I held his cooling hand and asked the two words spoken many times during our years together. "Now what?" This time there was no response. I was on my own for the first time. When my fingers touched his wedding ring, I slipped it off and held it in my fist. The gold band was warm. I clung to him. "Come back to me, dearest." Sometimes what you wish for is more than you can live with.

Reconstructing Charlie

Charlie Costigan has a secret. Home life gone from bad to the worst when she protects her mother from another vicious attack by her drunken father. Midnight. Clothes thrown into an old suitcase, she races for the bus with a letter to an unknown aunt and uncle. "This is my daughter. Embrace her as if she were your own." Determined, Charlie begins again. Alone with her secret.

Sin of Omission

A twist of fate intervenes when Shelley keeps a secret that threatens to break apart the Costigans and her future. A mysterious client, Deanna Rose, enters Haven, victim of a savage beating under strange circumstances. Shelley investigates and finds Ms. Rose has an unsavory past. With the reputation and safety of Haven at stake, Shelley is at risk to lose everything and everyone she cares about.

The Catch

Tom Donnelly, once known as The Catch – every woman's dream guy, has fallen down every rung of the ladder he once worked so hard to climb. On New Year's Day, he realizes just how far he's fallen, and makes a list of resolutions to change his life. He vows to regain the trust lost from his family, his law firm, and his friends – and maybe even find the right woman this time.

ALSO IN AUDIOBOOK!

The first three stories in the series of Mature Romance combined in one volume. Instant Grandpa, Book 1; Young at Heart, Book 2; and Before the Final Curtain, Book 3. These Charmaine Gordon stories of love, passion, and suspense starring sexy seniors are also available as singles in ebook.

Instant Grandpa, Book 1

Summer at the Jersey Shore just got hotter… Take one widower grandfather, add two little grandkids, and widowed grandmother with a small granddaughter. Mix well. Stir in sun drenched beach days and moonlit nights. What have you got? A kite flying high with a new tail; an author writing a book to sort out emotions; a talented boy with his mother returned to claim the prize.

Young at Heart, Book 2

Seventy year old Joyce Campbell expected her new left hip to heal at Helen Hayes Rehabilitation. What she didn't expect was to fall in love with the distinguished silver haired Collin Brody who wouldn't give her a second glance. Until Kizzy, the therapy dog comes into Collin's life…and into his heart. What happens next? The Beginning, Not the End.

Before the Final Curtain, Book 3

Once lovers, aging actors collide on stage as stars in a romantic comedy written and directed by a manipulative director. Add to the mix the talented assistant, a tough stage manager, one prominent costume designer, two young actors, secrets and gossip. Show business. There's no business like it.

ALSO IN AUDIOBOOK!

The next set of three stories in the series of Mature Romance combined in one volume. No Time for Green Bananas, Book 4; She Didn't Say No, Book 5; and Dr. D. and the Dad, Book 6. These Charmaine Gordon stories of love, passion, and suspense starring sexy seniors are also available as singles in ebook.

No Time for Green Bananas, Book 4

Celeste Hamlin, seventy-five year old widow, has a goal... conquer the six mountains in the Saranac Lake region before deciding what to do with the rest of her life. Sixty-two year old Professor Paul Harris, meets the dynamic Celeste, and recalls the last words his wife said before she passed. "Find another love and begin again." Will they begin again?

She Didn't Say No , Book 5

Grace didn't say no to the Big Man On Campus, Scott Dwyer. And then her life changed... Years later, a too-close encounter of an unpleasant kind with a skunk and Scott's German Shepherd reunites the former lovers. What happens in between are their stories of beginnings and endings and love lost, then found.

Dr. D and the Dad, Book 6

A trip over a mound of sand on the beach begins a journey for Diane O'Rourke and Tony Flannigan. She's a pediatrician, a bit over weight; he has a foster care home with three children under his sheltering wing... and a dark secret. Can they overcome the past and make the future work for them? They might just find the initial trip was well worth it.

Farewell, Hello

That first kiss... that first incredible, agonizing, bellyache-making first kiss. Soon, Joy and Danny are inseparable, planning a future – a life, together. A kiss goodbye couldn't prepare the high school sweethearts for all that lay ahead. A family crisis, a tornado, and the Korean War brought their plans to a screeching halt, and changed their futures... but maybe not their forever.

No Time for Green Bananas
The Beginning, Not the End, Book 4

Celeste Hamlin, seventy-five year old widow, has a goal... conquer the six mountains in the Saranac Lake region before deciding what to do with the rest of her life.

Sixty-two year old Professor Paul Harris, meets the dynamic Celeste, and recalls the last words his wife said before she passed. "Find another love and begin again." Will they begin again

Author Charmaine Gordon

Charmaine Gordon writes books about women who Survive and Thrive. Her motto is take one step and then another to leave your past behind and begin again. Six books and several short stories in three years, she's always at work on the next story. The books include *To Be Continued*, *Starting Over*, *Now What?*, *Reconstructing Charlie*, *Sin of Omission* and *The Catch*, and her series of Mature Romances, The Beginning...Not the End, including the stand alone novellas, *She Didn't Say No* and *Farewell, Hello*.

"I didn't realize at the time while working as an actor in NYC, I'd become a sponge soaking up dialogue, setting, and stage directions. I learned many tools of writing during the years watching directors like Mike Nichols and actors including Harrison Ford, Anthony Hopkins, and Billy Crystal. And would you believe, I was Geraldine Ferraro's stand-in leg model, my first job giving me entrée into all the Unions needed to work. When the sweet time ended, I began another career and creative juices flowed."

You can reach Charmaine at
http://AuthorCharmaineGordon.wordpress.com

And on her FB page http://www.facebook.com/charmaine.gordon

www.ingramcontent.com/pod-product-compliance
Lightning Source LLC
Chambersburg PA
CBHW070552130626
46556CB00001B/123